The Disturbing Workings of Chris Crow

Compendium of Horror: Volume 1

by

Chris Crow

DORRANCE PUBLISHING CO
EST. 1920
PITTSBURGH, PENNSYLVANIA 15238

Dorrance Publishing Co
585 Alpha Drive
Suite 103
Pittsburgh, PA 15238
Visit our website at *www.dorrancebookstore.com*

ISBN: 979-8-88925-158-3
eISBN: 979-8-88925-658-8

Contents:

The Disturbing Workings of Chris Crow

Mori

Her name was Kaitlyn Markwell. When she was growing up, she didn't receive much Divine intervention because she was always sick and often missed school. It seemed like the Gods wanted nothing to do with her and 'killed' her off before she was even a teenager. Kids teased her when they actually saw her. They called her awful names like "Lousy Drowsy" or even "Kaitlyn Never-well." "Kaitlyn Never-Well should go to Hell and take her sicknesses with her!" Kids would yell this and laugh at poor Kaitlyn. Kids aren't very creative, but kids can be the modern-day evil with the cruelty they exert and with the lack of morals that the parents teach.

She always ended up in and out of hospital beds until she developed immunities by age 12, around the time she experienced her first period. But by this time, Kaitlyn wanted to actually have friends besides the doctors, nurses, and the friends her mother invited, plus, the mother herself. She looked to interact with kids and teens of her neighborhood to find out kids don't communicate easily anymore without the help of a phone. She was decaying inside until her calling came knocking at the door. It was no one, but rather a message taped to the door like a "Wanted" job flyer.

It read as:

<u>Wanted</u>
In need of a babysitter who can watch our precious
boy from between the hours of: 9:00pm - 12:00pm.
We are offering payment of $12 an hour with bonus pay if
hours run over. We preferably want a young girl
who has experience dealing with kids.
We can be found at:
2115 Dixie Lane SW 4th Place Terrance Dawsonville, Oregon
<u>We hope to see you soon.</u>

"Obscure," she thought to herself, but she hadn't had much luck in her life, so she jumped with glee at the opportunity. She had experience with the younger patients at the hospital, so how hard could it be to cater to the needs of one infant? She loved kids and also loved to care for them. Kaitlyn read to the sickly kids at the hospital. She got joy out of seeing these kids actually enjoying themselves rather than seeing them wallow in their pain. She knew now what she was destined to do in this particular moment in her life. She was going to become a babysitter. So maybe now she could fill the void in her chest with caring for other kids rather than making friends; plus, the pay was great, too.

She had discussed it with her parents, and they were excited to see young Katie find a purpose rather than be moody and depressed, sulking around the house all the time. She would be finally out of the house and productive. Her parents didn't mind, and the house wasn't but a mere couple miles away. They drove her to the address of the house, and thought nothing of the lack of a phone number on the flyer.

The home was rather nice looking. The home was painted pink and olive curtains blocked the view of the inside. The only thing that was amiss was the lack of grooming of the yard. Weeds grew massively and in clusters around the yard. The grass almost towered poor Kaitlyn. This left Kaitlyn with an uneasy feeling that grew larger with every step as she approached the front door. She was scared, but that was natural of a young girl in a strange new place.

"Bye-bye, sweetie, we'll be around twelve to pick you up unless you text or call us otherwise," the parents bid farewell to their daughter, knowing that they left Dad's phone in the care of their only child, Kaitlyn. She was scared and felt a pit develop in her soul as she saw her parents drive off. She knew she wanted to do this, but felt unready. This feeling was unnatural to her even though she was now a teen and needed the courage of an adult to succeed. So she sucked it up and shortened the distance between her and the door.

She now stood in front of the door. Her heart was racing now as she wondered what would come of her if she rang the doorbell.

Riiiinnngg

No one answered…

Riiinnngg

No one answered again. Kaitlyn began to worry and wondered if she were not needed tonight.

Riiinnngg

The third time had to be the charm, but it wasn't. Kaitlyn was anxious and uneasy at the lack of presence in the home, but as Kaitlyn began to depart from the front door it opened slowly with a long unbearable creek as the doorway widened. "That's unusual?" she questioned as she began to change her direction. As she entered the doorway, her stomach sank, and she now knew she shouldn't be here. She didn't heed the internal warning that lay dormant in the pit of her stomach, though because her lack of friends left her lonely and in need of company, she needed this job.

The inside was dark, but lovely only because the antiques gave character. The antiques that covered the house looked old and collected more dust than the material it was made of, over-layering the surface. The wallpaper suffered water damage from the floor above and looked moldy and torn. The inside felt dense as if—in the air—spores from the mold lingered like dust. Kaitlyn tried to force the door open, but the door was formidable and unyielding, and breaking down the door wasn't an option with her weak exterior. She choked more harshly as she made her way through the house to seek out salvation, but besides the mold that affected her, she felt something lingering in the shadows.

The obscured house left nothing but imagination because the shadows that danced around her didn't feel friendly at all—instead, as she crept further in, dread washed over her. The butterflies swarmed violently in the pit of her stomach while her lungs suffered as well.

Cough

Cough

With the last cough, something flew past as Kaitlyn passed by the staircase that laid on the right of the hallway that led to the living room. She was shaking and on the verge of blacking out, stumbling. Her fear was the only thing keeping her conscious. She started to head back to the front door when she heard a sound coming from beyond the living room.

Waaa

Waaa

The sound was that of an infant crying...

"Wait! A child couldn't survive in these conditions!" Kaitlyn said with a gasp and a severe cough. Her insides were burning and pneumonia was setting in. She felt sick and dizzy, and walking soon became a problem. When she walked into the living room, something shuffled in the darkness. Her heart raced. The pain in her lungs nearly compared to the overwhelming panic in her chest that felt like her heart was on the verge of exploding. Tears overflowed from the fear, but she quickly pushed past the other hallway adjacent to the living room towards the baby's cries.

The hallway consisted of multiple bedrooms along the walls, but the cries sounded like they came echoing from the room at the end of the hall. When Kaitlyn rounded the corner, she noticed, with sheer disgust in her face, that a trail of blood swallowed the floor and led directly to the room with the baby's cries. "My God!" she yelped as she covered her mouth to keep quiet not to alert the being that stalked her from the shadows. But whatever lurked behind her now breathed down the back of her neck. Her fear left her in shock, and now she felt a stillness come over her. "What the Hell?!" Her heart pounded furiously as her body devoured her voice. She couldn't move due to a state of paralysis; she was paralyzed.

Then the creature spoke in what seemed like a multitude of tones with a whisper as it reached out to grasp Kaitlyn's shoulder, "Look dear, the babysitter is here." An icy chill and a kick of adrenaline pulsated within her, and now all she thought about was her own life until she heard the cries again. Her huffs of anxiety almost overshadowed her own cries. The hallway felt endless as it seemed that the hallway was extending as she pushed forward. She grew dizzy and tired and almost collapsed because her vision started to fail as well as her limbs. She was growing weak.

"Look dear, the babysitter is so keen on wanting to watch our baby," said the demonic fourth-dimensional voice as it trailed behind Kaitlyn who was nearing the door.

She slammed the door behind her with a swift, but almost nearly fatal, success. It would have been her to end if she were just a second off, for when it closed the monster clashed with the wood frame and knocked her on her ass. Her breathing was heavy, but she tried to calm down trying to swallow her spit, but rather choked on it instead. She rose to her feet to see she was in a nursery. Wood boarded up the windows letting in only a strand of light. The strand of light shown through the cracks, like an omen for it illuminated the crib that stood in the center of the cramped room. Extremely worn curtains drifted across the wood that boarded the windows. The wallpaper color faded to grays, and the black mold littered the walls. This is the room that birthed the spores that were fatal to Kaitlyn's health and lingered in the house like a poisonous gas cloud.

She then drew her eyes towards the crib. It was now the moment of truth. The silence was deafening. Not only was the creature at bay and silent at the door, but also the baby was no longer weeping. Dread washed over, and that was all she felt now. She slowly crept to the crib. The child was almost in her sight. The child was wrapped in an old, tattered pink blanket that covered its face. She picked up the infant. The baby's weight felt too light compared to average-sized babies. She slowly pulled the blanket up to reveal the face of the child, and with every moment that passed, the tension started getting heavy on her chest. Something felt wrong. Then with fear and a devastating shock, the face was revealed.

The child was a doll...

The doll was infested with mold and insects. The eyes looked burnt out and had cockroaches crawling in and out of the sockets. It was purely an impulse, but the hypothalamus sent a signal to the adrenal glands in her torso to send out cortisol and adrenaline to send that doll soaring into the wall opposite of her. The impact caused the mold on the walls to pulsate as if they were sentient, but instead something was actually emerging from the poisonous plant that formed across the wall. It was a grown child.

This child was not ordinary. The mold that infected this house was one with this child or came from this child. And it was a girl, roughly around the age of eight to ten. She wore a tattered dress that was once white but now just looked like the insides of the house. Her veins were black and popped out and crawled up her body, connecting to the mold that riddled her body. The left side of her face was black mold and the other actually showed her features. Her skin no longer held a pink glow like most people, but rather, she was gray with hints of green pigments, almost like a plant.

Kaitlyn lost all sense of motor skills and collapsed to the ground in sheer fright. She began to hyperventilate, causing immense pain in her chest. She coughed to reveal blood in her hand. She was on the brink of death, if not from the atmosphere, then from the threat that drew near. Her heart raced only to cause a sensation of blackouts. Death was drawing near, and that only intensified the fear. Then it spoke. "Shh-shh, no need to fear, it's nearly over. And you will no longer be alone. We'll be together forever." Her voice was so gentle and comforting as if she were an angel, but Kaitlyn knew what lay before her. This was a demon. A single tear rolled down her face before it wiped it away, gently caressing her cheek. "Now we can all be a happy family forever and ever and ever." Then the room grew dark, and its voice deepened as the room dimmed to pure darkness. The last thing Kaitlyn heard before her last moment of life was that of a giggle of a happy child.

Giggle

The next morning was that of pure sorrow and grieving. Kaitlyn's parents lay collapsed and broken in front of the residence where they last saw their dear daughter. They were being kept away from the abandoned home by law enforcement and hazmats. Hazmats walked out of the building carrying the remains of Kaitlyn, or what they believed to be her. Her parents broke down even worse and their tears formed a river. "Get back!" announced one of the Hazmats. Kaitlyn's remains were gruesome, she looked decomposed to the bone, and looked black like midnight covered in mold. Her face held a terrifying expression. Her mouth held open, gaping wide, as if her last moments were used screaming, and her arms stretched out of the mold that entangled around her. And her mom's last look at her daughter was that of her daughter reaching out as if she were calling for her mom with her dying breath…

"Mom?!"

Kanji

There is a cellar located deep in the woods. Woods so desolate that the fog alone is so dense that souls can't find their way home. Children get lost to never return, and I, too, now stand in front of the cellar that all find themselves when they enter these woods, 'The Devouring Oaks.' I say the woods feed on the lost and the cellar is the mouth.

The fog feels like an entity all on it's own; the dementing hold of the fog is like the arms of the woods that enclose around the frightened, and welcomes the meal. I could not see the trees until I was up on them. And all the trees looked burnt and brittle.

I'm frightened, but I had to find my sister. I followed her pace, but she managed to speed ahead even with her leg length being half the length of mine. How is that even possible? I believe she was snatched. And that's why I now stand at the foot of the cellar even if I backtrack or even move forward, I always end up back here.

My eyes a streaming waterfall and my chest a piercing sensation like a blade to the heart, I fear intensely for my sister, but when I go for the handle of the cellar, the butterflies in me begin to die and I fear that only death lingers in this hole.

"Jessie," I whimpered to myself. If what I'm feeling is true, "Oh God!" The tears were overwhelming as I lifted the massive decrepit door which felt strangely light. The weight of the door alone made my heart sink to the darkest thoughts as for my sister would have been able to open this door, too. The handle left a rusted stain upon my hand, and I noticed it was there as I made my way down into the blackest depths of the cellar.

The loud clicking sound of my heels matched my heartbeat within my chest as I steadily crept down the steps that descended into darkness. I couldn't breathe. The fear gripped my lungs and my aching pain bore fear's fruit. I ran out of tears while my eyes were so swollen and red.

But nothing could have prepared me for the gruesome sight I glimpsed when I reached the bottom. Whatever light peered from the cellar opening illuminated—barely—on the horrific display that laid before me. I threw my hands in front of my mouth and I began to go blind with tears. I felt dizzy and nearly passed out from the shock that left me dumbfounded with fear. I couldn't collect the courage or the bravery to run or pick myself back up. What I saw was my own flesh and blood feasting on human flesh; my little sis now was a monster.

She turned to stare at me. She was no longer human. Her mouth tore in half and no longer had teeth, but maggot-like beings burrowed into the holes in her gums. You could see the muscular layer of the jaw ripping open with every gruesome sound as the wormlike-maggots wiggled outward towards me. Blood just poured from my sister's mouth, and she couldn't speak but rather made clicking sounds. Her eyes were white as death, and with every movement, her bones made terrible cracking sounds that gave way to my teeth grinding and tears streaming from my face. As the monster and the creatures in her mouth closed in, my heart grew louder and louder until I felt nothing but my pulse… I was staring into the cold eyes of death.

I held my breath with my hand in front of my mouth trying not to alarm the monstrosity. But it grew harder as the cellar door began to shut. My heart started to pound louder even while my stillness hardened my stance like a statue. The tears were too much now, and the holding of my breath began to darken my sight. As the cellar reached pure darkness, I felt my lungs strangling me. I released a gasp for air, and in that instance, the creatures shot from my sister's mouth and into mine. I began to choke as the wormlike-parasites burrowed into my insides. Then the door sealed, and in the darkness, I could feel my jaw begin to rip in two as the blood soaked parasites burrowed down into my chest—then my stomach, feeling as they expanded throughout my internal organs claiming my body as just another host. They squirmed through my veins—my muscles—until I was a living puppet begging for death, but at least, I had my sister.

Mi Amore No

My love was always near, or at least I hoped. I may not live with her, but she does come get me often to spend all our possible time together. Her beautiful face—and with that smile—brightens my day when I'm feeling down or even when I just need its presence. I never cared for figures, but her curves can easily make the earth jealous. I hope I never lose her.

I awoke one dreadful night drenched in sweat and tears, but I didn't remember the cause. All that crossed my mind was that I needed my love by my side. The gloomy presence and darkness of the room still left me uneasy. I tried to go back to sleep, but the dread caressed over me as if the fear needed me. I laid awake until my lack of will left me, and I fell again to the dreamscape.

Next morning, my darling came to get me again for an evening out, and we just went to the movies to see the latest film. My heart raced and the feeling of love in me was overwhelming, and it felt as if my heart was spilling blood. I tried to hold her hand, but she was keener on the popcorn she wouldn't let me buy for her. This had never really been an issue. I never questioned my feelings for her, but the thought made my heart sink into the bowels of my chest. She could have had both: my hand and the deliciousness of the buttery popcorn. We didn't talk much after or before the film, but she did say, "Thanks, I had a great time." Those words made me smile. 'The night came too soon,' I thought as I was dropped off at home.

We both said, "See ya later," but I was the only one to say, "I love you."

Night. I dread the thought of sleeping again. I hadn't properly slept in days. I believed everyone noticed, but never really cared. My problems were my own, I know, but I would like a little concern from someone. My eyes sunk in, and there was a shade of black that lingered around my eyes. I lay in bed feeling the dread again—and hoped to have pleasant dreams, but that feeling of fear came over again so I laid awake until the time came. Then in that moment, it washed away as I saw my girl come into my room with the dark lingerie she loved to wear.

"Hey, need some company, 'Boo?'" she said as she bit her lip lustfully.

I welcomed this, and smiled passionately as she made her way to my bedside. I didn't think so much into the thought of why she was here, but that sense of dread returned as she approached closer. Why? I loved her. So why was I now afraid? I shook off these feelings now as she leaned in and passionately kissed me. I became aroused and that caused the blood to my head to go straight into my dick. The warmth of our bodies made me feel as if I were in a sauna. I groped her breasts, and then her back and laid her down. After that I began to move further south, but...

There was something wrong. The fear was pounding through my chest again, and my head set off alarms. I ask again, why? Then the answer came clear. When I rubbed her clit, it felt more unusual than any other because I swear it moved, so my eyes made their way down. My eyes widened, and in horror, I saw why my chest was exploding, and why the dread and fear remained. Her clit was replaced by maggots, and the vagina was being eaten alive. I could see them worming their way through as blood filled in the slivers of what was her vaginal cavity. Tears overwhelming in my eyes, I threw my hand over my mouth in sheer terror. My tears nearly blinded me, and the shock nearly caused me to blackout.

"Oh baby, I like when you touch me like that." She was enjoying the little monsters eating her out, and then I looked up to see her expression. She no longer had a face. Her face looked like smooth drywall. And her voice grew deeper like a demon. "Oh baby, you're an animal!"

I awoke. It was… It was a dream, a nightmare. I was drenched again like the other nights in cold sweat and tears. At least, I thought now I was safe in the land of reality, but then I received a text. It was my love. I was happy to see her messenger show one of her pictures until I actually read the message. It read, "I think.. I think that this isn't gonna work. I might not be pansexual, but actually only like girls. I'm gonna end up hurting you, and I think that I already am because I don't feel anything. I just… don't know what to do…"

I interpreted the meaning of my dream, and it was warning me the whole time. My relationship was dead inside, and all we had was the thought of being together. I saw now what the horror was: the inevitable demise of my love life. And now nothing remains of my soul.

In Extremis

It's inevitable, and I'm helpless. I stare at the stars to distract me from the roaring waves that surround my every side. And I'm not comfy on my bed that floats above the body of water. I'm in a frightening trance, or binding. I can't move a muscle, but I'm fully aware. All I have are the stars to occupy my gaze.

It's a pure pinching sensation that binds me down. You feel, but can't move. It's like I'm forced by an entity of sorts, but if I am, I can't see the being hovering over me. I'm terrified to think that the water's rising, and I may drown gasping for an early release from this life, to gag on the liquids forced into my lungs. If this entity that holds me is a demon, then this must be Hell. But Hell is equally as stunning as horrifying.

I hear the water clash against my bed and against themselves, but I still can't budge to see where I'm going, and if it is leading to Hell. For all I know, I could be on the verge of a fall even though I don't hear the roars of a waterfall. The fear of the unknown pulls at my heart, equally to my mind. I'm losing it, or should I say I already had. I don't recall how I ended up on this voyage across a vast ocean covered by night, and all I could see were the stars. All I know is without my movement sooner or later I'm dead.

I rapidly begin to hyperventilate. I tried to steady my breathing, but what binds me gets more terrifying as I finally begin to feel the water that kept me afloat. Then all of a sudden, voices cried out from the Heavens, but I've yet to make out the words. And this is where my courage, bravery, and need to live began to be tested when storm clouds began to form above. No longer could I see the stars.

I feel the waves and the rain as they harshly slam onto my face. I began to cry to myself, like the sky, as the thought that my lifeless body will begin to fall into the ocean, and I'll die a seemingly peaceful death with terrifying aspects. I would gag on the water that would replace the air that filled my lungs. I would see the last of my air leave in bubbles heading to the surface where I wish to be. But I'm still alive, so I shall not dwell on the possibilities.

Then a more frightening sight occurred in the sky. The dark menacing clouds began to form closer to me. Was it a hurricane? Am I to die so gruesomely? As these clouds began to form the voices grew more understandable, and replaced the thunder that should have rolled in with the unexpected storm.

"Stay with me!"

The voices came out clear now as lightning began to strike the seas around me. But that's not all. The clouds finally formed, and it wasn't a hurricane to be, but rather the entity holding me. My whimpers have changed to bloodcurdling screams. I could now move my body, and I was relieved, but the entity held me and began to push on my bed. It was going to drown me.

Its appearance was that of the sky. The dark clouds formed into a man with no face and its legs were a massive tail that led into the sky. This being held me tightly as I struggled with overwhelming tears pouring from my eyes. My back—now, laid in the ocean.

"Clear! We're not going to lose you!" The voices came from the entity. And as it finished its words, lightning struck right at my side. The jolt of electricity burrowed into the fibers of my flesh and pierced my heart. My tears ran dry because I was too much in shock now to gather fear or pain. The lightning was exhilarating! Light poured from within my chest, and the shade that blinded evaporated into nothingness—and the storm as well. But the light grew brighter and brighter until I no longer could peer at the ocean or even see the stars. I was now in a realm of light; nothing existed except for white.

…Then black.

"Awe, she's coming to."

I heard a voice as I came to. All was blurry at first, but I came to be able to see the face of the voice that came to my salvation. It was a man in a white coat, which held a name tag:

Dr. Matthew Greg
Louisiana Heights Hospital

More sounds and visions began to form around me. I heard the beeping of the machine, and I heard the general clatters of the hospital. Plus, I noticed the defibrillator that stood beside my bed.

But then the doctor began to speak again. "All your vitals are showing up fine, but I have to say, young lady, that you were dead for a very long time. I don't believe there is anything else we can do."

Wait! What did he mean by that?! The expression he held on his face was grim. That's when I noticed, I could only turn my head. I should have let that monster take me and drown me in the ocean because now all I can move is my neck up. My chest dropped with anxiety and dread as it came clear that I was paralyzed…

…From the neck down…

Dark Pheromone

The darkened mass of clouds covered the sky, revealing solely the moon and its stars in cloud breaks high above the woods on this eerie night. The trees rustled with a purpose as it seemed a storm was brewing with omens to come. The tragic night was the starting point of the fall of man for what was about to transpire would warp the very fabric of reality.

A small group of people laid deep in these woods; a small lumber camp of sorts owned by a major company started clearing out the woods to market the terrain for city expansion. Heavy equipment—now cold—rested as the workers rested as well for the night in a more obnoxious fashion. It wasn't very late, but it was around the late evening when the sun had set moments ago, and the moon now dominated the sky. Conveniently, the moon was full on this night of rejoicing as the workers held their own little party.

"To another day, and another dollar!" shouted cheerfully the Irish laborer whose hair burned bright like the fire they all gathered around. He raised his mug full of ale in celebration of the long hard day's work.

"Huzzah!" chanted one of the more burly workers who wore a massively round beard resembling a stereotypically iconic lumberjack. His flannel shirt laid halfway unbuttoned, exposing his untamed chest hair. He was quite the ladies' man of the group as well. After he raised his glass, he chugged his mug in one swig, slamming it down with pride.

"You shouldn't be drinking so hard. You know the workday begins again in the morning," said the rookie. Being in his late twenties and finally landing this job has made him reasonable and cautious of losing a great job. He was scrawny, but muscled, with a rugged, medium cut and a five o'clock shadow. He lingered in the back toward the tents that gathered around the flame.

"Awe, you're just a lightweight, Rook. Come party with the rest of us," said the only dark-complected woman on the team that cuddled up to the burly bearded man as she, too, raised her glass and cheered again.

"You know what, I think he has a point," said the Irish ginger that laughed loudly as he chugged the vodka like it was water, but that instantly backfired as he choked, resulting in a violent vomiting all over himself. He was now out for the count as he plummeted to the ground.

"Now who's the lightweight, O'Malley?" said Rook as if he were a smartass, and everyone just laughed.

Rook went to pick up O'Malley, but then he was interrupted. "Don't worry, he'll be fine. He literally does this every weekend," insisted the dark-complected woman, whose pigment was a dark caramel hue.

In the distance lingered a shadow of a man outside of the campfire party; he was the only black male of this branch, who also drank alone, in jealousy, while watching the bearded man fondle his ex. He didn't talk much; instead, he often came off as the tough guy being muscled up as if he had taken steroids, and wore a bald head and a goatee as a statement. Rook looked his way and saw his stare, and felt the cold of his glance, only forcing him to turn his gaze away quickly.

"Ah yea! Now this is a party," screamed a woman in the workforce. She was quite beautiful, and well-toned. Her hair shimmered blonde as her drunk self basked in the glow of the flames. "Come on, Hank, you need to drink more!" She latched herself around the burly man, swallowing rapidly the red wine she held in her hand.

"Trust me, Beverly, I've drank more than you. By morning, I'm going to be a living whiskey bottle." He laughed heartily with a rugged chuckle to his own joke. It didn't really look like anyone was paying attention other than Aaliyah, the black girl who snuggled him.

"Ha! Good one," she responded to Hank's lame joke.

The one that ignored everyone the most was the techie from across the flame that just read an article on his laptop using his hotspot from his cell. He often reads tabloids through the internet to keep up to date with possible weird things happening. He was the queer one in the group, being that he was in his early thirties yet still looked like a teen with his choice in haircut. He often hides behind his black hair. He also was the only one in the group that wore glasses.

"Mark, put down your technology, and have some fun, gosh," Beverly said while she jumped straight to him, barely holding her balance. She then lost her balance before being able to latch onto him, and tripped right over the log he sat on. "I'm good, " she mumbled with a thumbs up.

While everyone laughed by the fire, Rook approached the shadowed man who was chugging a Bud Lite with a purpose while he stared still so intensely at Hank. "River, why are you all alone over here? Get over it already, and join the party," he told River with a confident chuckle, only to shut himself down when he saw River's look he gave him.

"Fuck you say, Rookie?" It was a rhetorical question because clearly River held a death grip stare now towards him.

"Fine, be that way, I'm only saying things only get better if you let the wounds heal." He gave him a concerned look to combat his aggressive gaze.

"Just fuck off, she'll be back. They always come back," he finished with a chug of another beer.

"Denial isn't just a river in Egypt, River, but you'd know all about that." He walked off, leaving with a smart remark that doubled as a pun; he felt clever because it was a joke that was properly executed.

Rook left the shadows to finally join the group by the fire to bring the merry band back together, besides River: Beverly who laid now passed out on the floor cuddling what was left of her wine, Aaliyah who still hung out with her future man, O'Malley who Rook couldn't help but move him to his tent, and Mark who now poked and prodded the fire. While they partied, which they will regret in the morning, something was transpiring deep in the woods that carried on the wind—something sinister, something sentient. The woods now grew restless, and the wind reflected that unease with violent gusts. It picked up so suddenly, and the gang saw it as time to pack it up. Aaliyah said goodnight and carried Beverly to their tent, same as for the others. Mark was already in his tent by this point, and Hank had to finish his drink before he'd even try to remove his numb ass from the log. River just walked off into the darkness, and Rook didn't care enough to follow; instead, he also sought shelter from the possible storm that was on the rise.

River's self-loathing didn't cease. He kept the party going as he rapidly downed the last of his six-pack. In a rage, he shattered the bottle on the nearest tree with an unlikely precise throw. With the shatter, he yelled, but he couldn't be heard over the loud rustling of the trees and the drunken nature of his associates. Then the sound of wood crackling like that of it being in fire eerily presented itself above him making him look up so suddenly.

"What was that, something there?!" he roared at the sky which he couldn't see past the trees. The crackling only got louder, and it made him feel a sense of unease. "Leave me alone! I swear I'll cut you!" He patted himself down and pulled out a switchblade from his back pocket.

Then his eyes faced forward when he realized the crackling now came as snaps of twigs from in front of him. He became quite startled as his eyes jumped to the origin of the sound to see a shadowy figure stand before him. No more sound emitted from this being, but instead it stood there. It was unaffected by the wind that raged.

"Hey, shit-bird, this is private property! Turn your sissy-ass right around, and go on your merry way, bitch!" River threatened the figure in hopes of intimidating it into leaving. He was still heavily buzzed, and had no hope of a decent chance of taking anyone in a fight in his current condition, but the shadow stood completely unphased. He began to back up slowly while trying to keep his shaky vision straight. He wasn't exactly afraid because the drinks made him feel invincible, but he could barely walk, which kept him incapable of anything.

Then the shadow began to move closer, but it didn't even seem like it was walking. It carried itself in the air, no real movement. It phased through the shadows as it crept closer. River thought he was seeing things, and at this point he was terrified. His heart dropped and raced like a drum being violently beaten. The fear almost made him sober with the sudden kick of norepinephrine. In this response, he chose 'flight' because what he was seeing couldn't be explained.

But with a sudden burst, he ran in an instant back towards the camp, not realizing he wasn't running in the correct direction. Nothing looked the same as it did before, and the trees looked to be closing in. They weren't closing in as fast as the shadow that unresponsively floated behind though. An unnatural sound of wood crackling surrounded him as he pursued shelter from the horrors he endured. His heart raced immensely as if he were having a heart attack.

But the fear was all short-lived as he looked back for the last time, a branch piercing his chest the moment he did. His vision failed him, and all started to go black as blood shot out from his mouth. He tried to mutter a word, but the branch shattered his ribs and impaled his lungs. River was dead almost instantly. And with that, the shadow vanished.

The morning came—dawn broke, and the crew assembled in the mess hall for breakfast. Beverly wore her shades with purpose while she gripped her stomach in hopes of not vomiting, but Hank looked perfectly fine having the liver of an Irishman, unlike O'Malley who didn't have such a liver even being an Irishman himself. O'Malley burst into the double doors avoiding everyone while holding his mouth, and headed straight into the back corner towards the restrooms. Rook and Mark were already in the hall sitting across from each other, being the first ones awake because they hardly—if not— had consumed anything. They weren't exactly conversing. It was more like they enjoyed each other's company, both being self-proclaimed outcasts.

Then Aaliyah's booming voice burst through the hall with vigor. "Good morning, lightweights!"

"Ya, don't need to shout, princess," came O'Malley's voice as he hunched over at the bathroom archway.

"Like I said—lightweight, O'Malley in particular." She laughed with a smirk.

"Alright, ladies and ladies," the project supervisor raised his voice from the doorway leading to the kitchen, he said at first nodding toward the guys, and then towards the women with a more respectful gesture with his cowboy hat. As he continued toward the middle of the mess hall, he continued, " I need you all to assemble to one table for a head count, and your assignments."

"Well, isn't it always the same as every day?" snarkily O'Malley said as he sat, and gripped his head.

"For that, *Connor*, you're on landscaping duty," he responded with a smirk.

"God, I hate being in the sun as much as I hate seeing your ugly mug," he retaliated. It wasn't the smartest idea, but he couldn't help but get a kick out of annoying the supervisor.

"It almost seems like you don't want a job anymore, *Connor*," the supervisor then retaliated back with a more realistic realization than him being ugly, which he actually wasn't. He was a moderately chiseled young man who happened to be the son of the company's CEO. He worked hard to impress his father by proving he could rise through the ranks.

"Ah, shove it up your hole, you know you need me. Obviously, who would do your grunt work? You already gave me most of it."

"And you still complain more than Aaliyah, and she definitely works harder than you," he snickered, finishing off with O'Malley.

He then moved on to Aaliyah being that he mentioned her name. "Well, you already heard your tasks for the day, same as O'Malley."

"Yes, Sir," she acknowledged right away with no fight.

While that conversation was going on, Rook and Mark were having one of their own. It started when Rook said to himself quietly, but loud enough Mark could hear, "Wait, where is River? I didn't see him come back last night."

He looked around nonchalantly to see when Mark answered, "I noticed that, too. He should've returned because of the freakish storm last night."

"I know, right? But he was furiously jealous that Aaliyah moved on from him." Rook stood, puzzled by this realization. "He couldn't have gone to town because you'd need company permission to drive the vehicles."

"Maybe he's passed out heavy out there in the woods somewhere?" Mark answered with a question.

"That's probably it."

Then as the supervisor's conversation wound down from insult to insult, it, too, occurred to him that River was missing. "Wait, where is River? I had him scheduled to work the Backhoe today," he questioned as he swept through the papers on his clipboard.

"He might still be sleeping it off in the woods. He didn't come back last night," Rook interjected.

Hank just ate his breakfast, ignoring everyone around him while Beverly wobbled around with her shades, still on hoping not to vomit at the table she sat at. O'Malley sat next to Aaliyah in front, being the center of attention, because O'Malley wanted to mess with her, and Aaliyah always played the kiss-ass hard working employee. Rook and Mark were furthest from the group, Mark continued on his laptop while Rook continued with the conversation at hand.

"If River doesn't show up in the next five minutes, he is going to be transported to the nearest landmark, and fired from the workforce!" The supervisor was furious because this wasn't the first time he had done this.

"But Francis," he gave Rook a glance when he mentioned his name, "I mean, Sir, what if he had wandered off, and just lost his way, just passed out somewhere in the woods?"

He thought about what Rook said, and he gave River the benefit of the doubt. "Fine," he sighed while rubbing his neck as if he were stressed, which he could have been. "Okay, this doesn't count as company hours, so let's fan out in parties of two to search for River. He couldn't have gotten far, and no vehicles were tampered with because all keys were accounted for," Francis pointed out as loud ruckus from the kitchen workers sounded out as the other branches of the workforce were about to file in for their breakfast.

"Okay, listen up because breakfast is coming to an end, and the other workers will be filing in at any moment. Rook, since you were so keen on volunteering, I'm pairing you up with Aaliyah. Hank you are with *Connor*. I feel you can keep him on task. And finally, Mark and Beverly, you'll wait at the tents, and wait for River there, just in case he returns. I'll be passing out talkies to each team. Signal when you find him. We are not wasting more than an hour searching either, got it?!" When he finished, everyone acknowledged him with nods or vocal acknowledgment. "Now follow me outside so the other workers can eat." They assembled out front of the mess hall and moved toward the left side to hand out further instructions.

"Okay, Mark and Beverly, you already had your instructions, so I'll begin with you, Rook." Francis directed his gaze to the newest member of his force. It always seemed he sought more out of him even though he hadn't been here very long.

"Sir! Ugh, may I ask, Sir, but why do you all keep referring to me as Rook? It's almost as if all you had already forgotten my name?" It was a question that was sitting with him for a while.

"You're new. That is customary, I believe, to acknowledge you as such, but if it bothers you so much, *Brandon*, I'll refer to you as thus," he answered back in a mocking but stern tone.

"No, I guess it's fine. It never bothered me anyway," Brandon (AKA Rook) backed down.

"Good, Rook, we weren't going to stop anyway." Francis chuckled with a snicker from the rest of the bunch.

"Okay, can we get this going already?" O'Malley interrupted the fun.

"What, you in such a hurry to get back to work? Last thing I thought I'd see is O'Malley wanting to work," Hank mocked while Connor gave a disapproving look.

"No more bickering! Now, Rook and Aaliyah will go north while Hank and O'Malley will take the southside. And Beverly and Mark, you already have your orders," Francis interjected.

They all acknowledged him in one way or another with a nod, with a chant, or a disapproving grunt—O'Malley. They went their separate ways in their search for River.

· · ·

Rook and Aaliyah headed toward the woods past the work site their branch was in charge of. They started with calling out to him to get his attention in hopes the mission would end sooner than later. But then Rook broke the tension between personal and work-related. "Aaliyah, are you doing this because it affects your job or is this something different like you are worried for him?"

Aaliyah did hold a concerned look on her face. "I mean, I do care about my job deeply, but I did have a past relationship with River. I just—I don't know if this is just my fault or if—"

Rook then interrupted her in an attempt to console her, "You aren't responsible for his behavior. His choice is his choice. You won't be the reason he lost his job. He walked out on his own."

He held good points, and she knew that, but she just held a sinking feeling deep in her chest. "Let's not get into it, we need to find him, nothing more."

They continued walking, getting deeper and deeper into the woods, keeping quiet because Rook knew Aaliyah's mind was fragile right now due to the fact she believed this was her fault, toying with River's emotions. But then Rook couldn't help himself but to console her further, "I'm sorry to bring up the issue, but, Aaliyah, you care for Hank. I can see that. So why do you care so much? You are so happy with Hank."

He was going down a dark path bringing this to light. "Just drop it, I know you're right, but I can't help feeling guilty that I ended it on such harsh terms," Aaliyah responded with a sunken face of dread. "If something happens, I would solely feel responsible."

He realized that there was no consoling her. She was lost to worry, but the moment he started to utter a word, a screech like a banshee soared through the air. Aaliyah bursted into tearful screams as she dropped to her knees suddenly. He began to look up toward what startled her, and when his face stared straight up past the sunshine, River hung impaled above their heads.

• • •

Hank and O'Malley headed past the terrain being worked by the other branches of the workforce, making no eye contact as they stayed on task. They were already dealing with more than a search and rescue. "You know you're a right bastard," O'Malley jumped in all of a sudden.

"And why is that?" Hank questioned with a humorous look on his face.

"That! You don't take me seriously." He pointed at Hank with accusation.

"You know, I don't even think you take yourself seriously." He chuckled out loud, making sure O'Malley heard him.

"Like I said, right bastard, you even took Aaliyah from me, " he said, almost sad.

"Bro, you can't lay claims on a woman. The woman chooses you, maybe if you were more mature than she'd have an interest, but instead of having a humorous personality, you are a joke," he advised him.

"Whatever." O'Malley backed down, and just shrugged it off before he lunged with words, "I am who I am. No one can change their nature like a tiger changing stripes."

"Sure, buddy, whatever helps you sleep at night." He patted O'Malley on the back with a single thrust. "We need to continue forward. We don't have much longer before we have to get to work. Let's just focus on finding River." O'Malley just nodded.

• • •

The surroundings weren't quiet with all the tools and machinery going, but the tents were at least quieter than the direction that Hank and O'Malley went. Mark and Beverly patiently awaited River at the campsite.

Mark continued on his laptop like always as if his laptop held his true work.

"Do you ever put that down?" Beverly said, feeling annoyed as she started to sober up from her hangover. She pulled off her sunglasses when she finished mocking Mark.

"Well, if you must know, I do more than just my work here. I'm working on research. I don't believe you'd be able to even comprehend it anyways, but that's not why you're attacking me now. I know you're just anxious for River because you have a 'caring heart,'" he said, Beverly unaware if he truly meant that. He knew she was only directing her worries at him.

"Thanks, I really appreciate it." Her worries were merely distracted for an instant, "Yeah, I do care. I just hope he's okay. I've never known River to be gone this long."

"Well, trust me, we'll find him, or he'll come back." He started to go in for a pat on her back, but retracted and scratched his own head. He wasn't all too confident in himself if River would come back. His research on the area had shown that dangerous animals roamed the woods like black bears or even wolves.

"Well, all we can do is wait until we have to get back on the clock." She honestly wasn't too keen on working, but at least this search prolonged her suffering—so she'd have a chance to sober up before said work.

• • •

Rook hurried to shield Aaliyah's eyes from the horror, but she only laid crippled to the spot she fell. "You shouldn't see this!" he stated, taking a strong stand toward protecting her from the horrors above her.

She only cried uncontrollably while in shock. "This is my fault." She repeated this as a chant, over and over again.

Rook grabbed the walkie to alert the others to his whereabouts, but the moment only grew stranger. The sky instantly started to swell in a madness of black as clouds covered the skies. He just looked up while saying under his breath, "What the fuck?" Same went for all the rest of the workers; they all just stopped to stare at the eerie events that were unfolding.

Before anyone could get on the walkie, especially Rook, Francis broke the awe. "Everyone hurry back now!" Then the walkie just cut off. The sky continued to swirl in black clouds, and now the sun manifested into a blood moon, ominous things started to transpire. The changing of the sky brought what seemed like an EMP toward communication devices because no one now was able to communicate, and the same seemed for the vehicles for construction halted abruptly.

Rook broke out of the trance first. Aaliyah still remained in shock as her head now stared at the ground with tears just pouring out without a sound. "Aaliyah, this doesn't look good. We have to go and meet up with the others." She didn't move even though he started to tug on her shoulder to snap her out of it. "I can't leave you here. Come on! We have to go. There is something really fucked up going on here, and we're not sure if a storm's coming or if it's far worse!"

His begging fell on deaf ears. Was the shock too great or did she really blame herself? Was she using Hank just to make River jealous of whom she still loved? Rook puzzled this just for a second. He used all his might he could muster, and he lifted her up for a piggy-back ride. She didn't object; she laid limp and lifeless. "I guess I'll just have to carry you then," he grunted as they made their way back to the mess hall.

• • •

After Francis was cut off, Hank tried to respond but to no success. "What's going on? Do you read me?"

As they heard no sound coming from the walkie, O'Malley jumped in, "Give it a rest, obviously the damn thing is broken, dammit."

"For once, I guess you're right," said Hank, being a smartass.

"What do you mean for once?" O'Malley retorted.

"We should hurry back," finished Hank when he realized everything around them grew strangely quiet.

"You hear that?" Hank whispered.

"No," O'Malley answered back.

"Exactly, there is nothing."

"How is that?" O'Malley sounded concerned.

"I don't know, but I don't hear any of the other workers either. It's peculiarly quiet, and I don't like that they just up and vanished." Hank puzzled with an annoying, nagging feeling of uneasiness.

"You're absolutely right. I wonder what happened?"

"I don't know, but we should remain cautious from here on out." Hank made it relevant because he was looking out for him.

"Right, but this is some freaky shit," O'Malley nervously stated.

"Just follow behind me," Hank commanded.

"No hair off my brow, you'll work as a great shield,' O'Malley snickered.

Hank gave him a look as they started towards the mess hall. They treaded carefully, but their hearts only raced with unease.

$$\bullet \quad \bullet \quad \bullet$$

The one who didn't handle these events well, besides Aaliyah, was none other than Beverly. She suffered from lilapsophobia, which is a fear of hurricanes or tornadoes. The sky only shot her back to when she was young, so after Francis was cut off and Mark couldn't make the walkie work, Beverly started to tear up. With a hysterical burst of fear, she yelled, "We need to get to a shelter. Stop tinkering with that goddamn thing. It's obviously broken!"

Beverly ran off towards the mess hall with a dash. Mark called out to her in protest, "Wait! We must stick together." But she only kept running. Her heart raced rapidly like a double kick drum, and her panting cries carried on in panic. She wasn't thinking about anything but herself. Mark closed his laptop, put it away calmly, and muttered under his breath, "Well, it's your funeral." He finished with getting up and walking off.

Beverly nearly reached her destination when her glasses fell off her person. She didn't pay any mind to a simple and cheap accessory. When she reached the mess hall, no one had arrived yet before her. She flung the door open with force, and slammed it right behind her as she tried to catch her breath. Her gasps of breath were accompanied by whines. Tears swelled up in her eyes, but she choked them back as best as she could. Then she heard a crash from behind her. She darted back around just to assume the noise came from the kitchen area.

She was terrified, so she didn't utter a sound, but instead covered her mouth as she shimmied across the wall. Her stomach felt empty as her soul sunk deeper into the void. It didn't help that this freak, ominous storm knocked out all the lights as well, but it also seemed to take everyone with it. Since Beverly was seeking help alongside a shelter, curiosity gave way to her. She slowly inched her way to the kitchen to seek out the sound she heard moments ago. She desperately yielded to the hope it was a friendly face.

Then as she grew closer to the window that separated the hall from the kitchen, the being that created the sound became more visible to her. It was horrid. She clenched herself in terror, and slid down along the wall, quickly and quietly, to make herself hidden in the shadows as she made her way to the tables that riddled the hall.

The creature looked cautious as it moved out of the kitchen, and into the hall from the doorway that lay inches from the window it just walked past. Its head was grotesque as if it were torn in two. The skin was ripped from the mouth to the ear. The jaw just hung suspended as blood poured down all over the black trench coat it wore. It didn't stumble even though it looked to be in pain, and in its hand it gripped with intensity a massive butcher knife.

Beverly only covered her mouth, trying not to cry, as snot started to leak out from her nose. She started to silently crawl alongside the tables trying to find a fork, or perhaps a knife or something, to defend herself from the abomination that laid before her. It crossed her mind she could sneak out the front and run back into the storm, but what fear overpowered her more?

Her stomach felt sour and her nose was now stuffy, but that didn't slow her down. What started to slow her down though was her vision beginning to go black; too much of a shock of adrenaline can cause the body to fail. It wanted to fall—and wavered, the fear was too much, but if she stopped now, she'd perhaps die or pass out. Then due to her starting to lose her balance, she bumped into the table she was crawling alongside. Her tears started to swell again, and her breathing started to hasten as the footsteps started toward her direction.

The creature was shockingly calm as it gradually made its way toward her. How could something that was bleeding profusely keep such a level head? This was her moment, she managed to find that weapon she longed for. It was in that moment that her flight or fight response decided on fighting as she gripped the knife with desperation.

She jumped out in a sprint. Breathing heavily, she held the handle of the knife to her stomach as she gripped it with both hands. The creature turned around quickly the second she closed in.

Stab

Beverly's eyes widened as if she saw a realization as she entered death's door. The butcher's blade pierced her heart as she managed to get his gut, and then she fell with a loud thump.

• • •

The sky only continued to swirl with an ominous aura as Hank and O'Malley trudged through the woods. They felt as if they only had circled around a dozen times as they tried to make their way to the mess hall.

O'Malley was only getting more irritated as the walk just felt like an endless masquerade of what it actually was, a distorted stroll.

"We're getting nowhere! Where are we heading? We only keep ending up at the lumber yard," O'Malley protested from behind Hank.

"I know. I don't get it either. We only continue straight. How aren't we at the mess hall yet?" It even started to sound as if Hank were getting irritated

35

even though he is one of the more level-headed of the gang. "Well, wait... I have an idea. I know this might sound insane, but what if we just head deeper into the woods?" He concocted an abstract solution to their problem.

"Are you serious? We are already going in circles, and you want to get even more lost?!" O'Malley seemed not to approve of this lunacy.

"Hear me out. Something fucked up is happening anyway. We're going the right way, but only end up back where we were at. So, we need to look at it from an abstract point of view. If we do the opposite, we may get another possibility. The definition of insanity is doing the same thing over and over again expecting a different result, so let's break the cycle," Hank came off as wise as he made a logical point.

"I mean, I guess you have a point, " O'Malley buckled under the logical solution.

They both started back the way they came in hopes that it might be the right way. "This storm is something sinister, something supernatural almost." Hank began to question the situation entirely.

"You took the words right out of my mouth. It continues to make me feel uneasy, and it started out of nowhere in clear skies," O'Malley concurred, and added on to what Hank was already saying. They made their way back into the woods only to recognize where they were at as a new part of the woods entirely. "Wait!? I don't recognize any of this at all!" he burst out, now freaking out. "We were just by the backhoes. How'd we get here?"

"I don't know, but this shit is getting tiresome," Hank agreed with an irritated statement. Then they came across a figure off in the distance. It was huddled on the ground and cloaked in white. It turned out to be a man as they approached cautiously, and a scientist at that. He was checking out the flora in the area, or at least that's what they put together. "Hey, sir! Can I ask what the fuck you doing on private property?!"

The scientist paid no mind to them, ignoring them while he took some of the plant life and put it under a microscope. He illuminated the area with an old-fashioned oil lamp concerning that the electronics in the area didn't work. "Hey! My friend here was talking to you, you arsewipe," O'Malley jumped in.

Then the scientist answered, revealing his aging face and glasses with a calm demeanor, "Can you keep it down? I'm trying to focus. Your rambling is only hindering my work. Now go on, Neanderthals, my work needs tending to unlike your needless bantering." The scientist came off as a selfish, rude old man with no intention of paying any mind to them, but they were having none of that.

"No, like he said before, we're going to need an explanation!" O'Malley continued before Hank could say what he was trying to get out.

"Okay, Connor, calm. I just want one thing if you're not going to discuss why you are here. I want at least your name." That was a simple demand of him from Hank, but he actually started to give more than his name.

"Well, I completed the collection of this specimen, so I can at least give you what I know. I'm Doctor Daniel Gluberman, and I have been sent here to study the paranormal anomaly that's happening in these woods to see if it is dangerous to the surrounding areas or if it is limited to only this region." The doctor seemed to be earnest in his decision to tell them. "And you're all in danger. Nothing you see is real, generally. I have come to understand that the sky is still bright as day, but the images you see are merely a hallucinogenic property created by mutated spores—I believe—is created by this strange black flower I stumbled upon."

It seems the scientist was keen on showing his discovery. After new discoveries, possibly most scientists, doctors, or people in general tend to have that urge of needing recognition. Then Doctor Gluberman stood up to put his instruments back in his bag that lay beside him. "Well, that concludes my research of this area."

Then O'Malley lunged after suffering a state of shock at the realization of what was going on around here. "What are you saying? Are you all saying we're infected with a spore that is affecting how we perceive things?" It almost seemed like he was stuttering. He had cut off Hank before he could utter the same question, but he had another question instead.

"What can we do to cure or even prevent what's happening to us?"

"You can't. Well, not right now—"

A rustling randomly sounded right behind the scientist in the middle of his answering. It was a root that then tore itself out of the ground and wrapped itself quickly, and with force, around the scientist. It yanked him swiftly into the woods right behind him, and he became lost to the darkness.

Hank and O'Malley screamed in shock with a consistent, "Oh shit!" The incident was so fast that it caught them all off guard. "What the fuck are we going to do now!" O'Malley was quick to shout out profanity.

"Well, I guess all we have now is to try to find our friends before something terrible happens, who knows how bad these hallucinations are affecting them," Hank said with a sense of worry.

• • •

Rook managed to carry Aaliyah through the woods without hindrance besides having to lug her a good distance. He set her down on the front deck of the mess hall where she still was in shock, sobbing silently, and staring into the distance. "Aaliyah, you're safe, but I can't tell you what happened to River. I—I can just say, I at least won't leave you alone—"

Thump!

He was interrupted as he tried to communicate with the now catatonic. He was startled for a second at the random loud thump that sounded from inside. He wasn't sure how to react. Was it someone in trouble? Did someone fall? He had to know. He needed to know. The curiosity crashed through the gates of his heart. "Wait here, Liah, that could have been one of our friends. I'll be right back." She didn't respond.

He steadily worked his way to the door, and started with a call hoping for a response. "Hello! Anyone in there? I heard a loud noise," he said as he moved inward. "Are you injured?" When he entered, it was immensely dark on the inside. He could only see what looked like a figure that shuffled toward the bathroom, or at least he thought he saw. But this distraction tore him from watching his step, and he then came crashing down on something that he happened to trip over. He landed hard on the floor behind this obscured object, but when his eyes finally adjusted to the dark, he was met with horror. Right beside him was none other than his friend Beverly. Her eyes were lifeless and milky, and her face held the tears she cried long dried up.

Rook now laid in a pool of her blood. He was purely in shock, and felt a sense of disarray. He almost wanted to vomit because of the massive dread that now overwhelmed him. But before he could do anything, Aaliyah let out a bloodcurdling scream. As her bright red eyes couldn't produce any more tears, she said, "No, not Beverly. What fucking Hell is this!?" She became hysterical. " We... We need to find the others. If we don't, I don't even want to think who'd be next."

While she had her fit, and finally broke from her shock and switched it to anger, Rook realized not just one puddle of blood remained at Beverly's side, but rather, another puddle trailed off from hers as well. "What the hell?" he said, realizing it led toward the restrooms, where originally the figure he thought he saw moments ago had run off to. He stood up, and Aaliyah offered to help. "Aaliyah, stay close. I believe what did this may be still here" he told her while sneaking toward the restroom, keeping her right behind him.

"What do you mean?" she questioned, calming down now because her anger started to waver towards fear.

"See this trail of blood right here, this trail here is leading straight towards the restroom, and I swear to you I saw someone here when I first entered scuttle away," he explained in a whisper as they neared the entrance to the men's room.

He held a finger in front of his mouth indicating her to be quiet as they moved in formation into the restroom. When they entered it came as a shock, the lights flickered in and out like that in a general horror situation, like in the movies. But the question was: why are the lights working now when they had trouble moments ago? Then in an instant static interference screeched from the walkie they kept. Rook saw this as an opportunity to call out to his friends. "Hey! Can anybody hear me? The walkies seem to be working." He waited a second. "Hello?"

The walkie screeched once again causing Rook's heart to jump, and so he dropped the walkie, causing it to slide to the middle stall. Aaliyah, too, jumped at the spontaneous omen that transpired. The moment that the walkie started to stop grinding the floor's surface, it started to speak through the static. "You're not alone. The woods are watching. You are not getting out alive." The voice started out as a young girl that held a twisted disposition about her, and then got deeper toward the end of the statement.

Rook walked toward the walkie cautiously, but when he went to pick it up, it abruptly died. It gave him pause as he realized that the stall he now crouched in front of was exactly where the blood trail led. Quiet groaning and moaning came from within. A pool of blood lingered under the stall door as he noticed two feet that sat inches away. Then a mass burst from the door, tackling him. He fought to keep this being from hurting him, and in that moment of struggle he realized he was fighting Francis.

A massive kitchen knife hung only inches from his face. He could feel the drip from its tip fall rapidly across his face while the blood from Francis' gut seeped into his clothes. "You'll not get me again, monster! I'll kill you! I'll rip out your throat!" Francis screamed in desperation as he seemed to be fighting for his life, what was left of it. His face looked pale from the loss of blood, and his eyes sunken in. He looked terrified as if what he was seeing was some monstrous beast.

"Francis! Snap out of it," Rook desperately called out to reason with his crazed attacker. "Help me, Aaliyah! Something is wrong!" Aaliyah was struck with shock, and she couldn't manage to budge even an inch.

"I... I..." She tried to utter a sound, but it didn't seem to want to come out.

Rook managed to sway the blade from his face, but Francis still held the advantage, being the one on top. With a quick thrust, using all his weight, Francis shoved the blade into his shoulder. "Aaaahhh!" he screamed in agony, and Aaliyah only just fell, losing her nerve to stand.

But at that moment, a leg came crashing swiftly into Francis' stomach. It was Hank. He came with a sprint when he heard the struggle developing in the restroom, but the scream made him choose fight over flight when he heard his friend in need. O'Malley comforted Aaliyah as Hank stood at Rook's side in defense of a possible retaliation from Francis.

Francis stood to the best of his abilities, gripping his side where the wound was. The blade now dripped with the blood of Rook as he began to cackle. It was harsh, almost dead, with no force behind it. That was because he was practically dead himself. He fell to his wounds as he uttered one final word under his breath, "Demon." He now laid in the remaining pool of his blood.

"So that's the bastard that fucking killed Beverly?" O'Malley cried as he spoke a rhetorical question.

"What the fuck was that?" Rook groaned through his teeth from the pain as Hank helped him up.

"Why… Why would Francis kill Beverly?" Aaliyah spoke before anyone else could question it.

"Okay, you all are going to need to be caught up," Hank said with the intention to reveal what they discovered in the woods.

He began to discuss it with the help of O'Malley as a witness. Rook and Aaliyah were shocked to hear that the very forest around them was driving their friends mad with the release of mutated spores, and that it isn't certain if anyone they knew were alive, or if they would be able to be communicated with. They could easily see them as monsters, too, like Francis had.

Crash

Then a loud sound came from the kitchen, it sounded like the clashes of pots and pans. "What the Hell?!" everyone said almost identically to the shock. "I'll lead the way this time, you watch Rook, and we'll go see what that was," O'Malley commanded, feeling the need to be the brave one now.

They followed calmly and quietly out toward the noise, but then they saw something odd, a bright light illuminating from the darkness of the kitchen. They crossed the mess hall staying close to the wall, and slowly opened the door to the other room. The kitchen was a horrifying sight, all the chefs and even other members of the branches that worked here sprawled across the floor in a grotesque bloodbath. " Holy hell…" O'Malley said as he was the one who opened the door. As they all tracked in, they gave similar reactions: Aaliyah gasped holding her hand in front of her mouth, Hank looked to get a foul whiff of the stench of death, and Rook only continued to groan in pain.

What illuminated the kitchen that silhouetted the bloody display was a computer laid wide open. Whoever was here left in a hurry after stumbling causing the crash of dishes. Pots and pans and other instruments are scattered around the red array. Bodies were merely inches from each other, and they carried weapons clenched in their hands, some even held eyes or even tracheas ripped from their assailants. It was gruesome, and nearly made O'Malley hurl as he made his way to the computer.

It was a laptop, but not just any laptop. It looked familiar, like they had seen it every day since the day they worked there. This device was the property of one of their friends, Mark. Where is he now? Why did he run? Did he, too, see something horrific? On the screen lay a moving image that is silhouetted in black and white cells like that in any living tissue.

It looked like a constant screensaver as it seemed to replay, but in actuality, it was displaying a horror that played out before their very eyes, cells devouring cells. "What is this?" O'Malley held a look of horror on his face as he saw the plant cells grow continuously carnivorous against the animal cells in the images on the screen. The plant cells metaphorically resembled a lion devouring a gazelle as they chased down each cell in unison taking them out one by one.

"This is not good," Rook interrupted O'Malley's state of shock while being patched up by Hank. "By the looks of it, the plant cells are embodying the animal cells."

"What do you mean?" Aaliyah got out before Hank could, so he just continued on Rook's wound.

"It's just as it looks. Nature must have evolved, and it's now fighting back. The spores are probably more than just hallucinogens, they are breaking us down little by little. Our cells are being consumed by the Earth. You could say we're poisoned."

The fear they all felt at the realization Rook bestowed on them left a state of petrified terror on their faces. "That's fucking bullshit!" O'Malley raged as he slammed his fist down inches from the laptop. "So we're just waiting to die?! We need to find that bastard Mark, and we get answers from this motherfucker straight from the horse's mouth! Or I say we just kick this arsehole's fucking teeth in!" He was heated, channeling his fear into anger, rather than despair.

Then unexpectedly Rook agreed. "I agree. This is probably the best bet," he finished, not knowing that both Hank and O'Malley knew of someone else who could know the answers, or even be involved.

"There is another opinion though. We could even seek out the scientist we met earlier out in the woods before arriving here. He was possibly looking into making a cure," Hank had to mention.

"You don't know that!" Aaliyah burst out. "And for that matter, you have no idea what's out there. We don't know what's real. We fucking killed Francis, for God's sake!" She was being hysterical.

"No, we didn't. He succumbed to his wounds that looked to have been inflicted by Beverly," Hank interrupted her. She just burst out crying at Beverly's name. She ran out of the kitchen, out the back door. O'Malley thought to comfort her, but there was only one who could, "Just watch Rook here, Connor. I got this," Hank said while laying a hand on O'Malley's shoulder to acknowledge him to stay put.

Hank walked out the back as well to comfort Aaliyah. "Why? Why are we even still alive? And another thing, River wasn't even killed during this. It was before. What did he even have to do with this?" Aaliyah grew even more hysterical with every sentence she spoke. She held a point within her tear-stricken rant.

"Wait?! River is dead?" Hank shouldn't have been surprised, but he was still. "I had nothing against the guy, but you want to talk about it?" He was definitely concerned for her well-being. He knew she still had some feelings for River—or once had remaining emotions that lay on the heart like scars.

He sat beside her on the back steps to give her warmth, but not too close to seem like he wanted more. He always held a warm heart for others, but it was also obvious they both held feelings for each other. They were casually flirting for a week or so now, but now who is to say how long any of them have?

"I know he came off as a dick sometimes, but it's only because of how much he cared for you." He put a hand on her shoulder.

"He wasn't the nicest guy, and I hated him sometimes, but no one deserves what I saw was done to him." Her emotions showed through her teeth as she clenched them, trying to hold back tears. She went on to describe the scene she saw to Hank about how River was displayed like a message, which made him realize something.

"I see, that only means perhaps the woods are more alive than we last thought, or at least I thought. O'Malley and I saw back in the woods the scientist get dragged off by a root or something, but perhaps if that happened to River as well, then maybe this was premeditated. Perhaps, we are the real study?" He finished with a wild speculation.

"That's shite!" O'Malley interrupted as he pushed his way out the back with the laptop in its case draped over his shoulder, along with Rook as he helped him out. "It has to be Mark who is behind this shite! I'm going to take this bloody laptop to the authorities, and bring that bastard to an end!" He held a vendetta, but he was missing one crucial fact about the events of today.

"What you are saying may be true, but you are forgetting about the scientist," Hank spoke clearly, and with a hint of concern. "It's not known who is actually behind this."

"The scientist?" Rook struggled to talk. The wound was quite painful.

"We saw the fucker die, didn't we?!" O'Malley believed his eyes when he saw the revelation transpire before him moments ago.

Then Aaliyah spoke out, and interrupted Hank before he could concur. "Yes, you did mention that none of this could be real." She stared blankly forward before turning slowly toward everyone, and spoke, "You didn't mention a body. I saw River hanging there—dead—but you didn't mention anything about seeing anything gruesome besides a damn tree." She then stood up and turned to them. " We need to return to where the scientist was. It's not guaranteed if either one isn't involved. We have enough proof of that." Her fear gave way to what seemed a burst of reasoning, or perhaps, even being stuck in her mind opened her third-eye to the answer they sought.

Hank was surprised as much as the rest. It was the best chance they had. "I, in the midst of all this chaos, didn't even realize this. I was too concerned about you guys. I didn't even think of that, even after all the scientist told us."

"Then I guess where we are going is back into the danger." Rook chuckled, even though it caused him pain. Hank led the charge. O'Malley continued to care for Rook, giving him the pain meds he needed as the time came, and Aaliyah trailed behind.

"Be wary. We aren't sure of what's out here," Hank stated the obvious. The wind blew with intensity, but not in a hindering fashion. The woods rustled with ominous intentions as he halted the party. "Before we move any further, we should better arm ourselves. It's not known if we'll run into more crazies like Francis. I know it's horrible to think we may end up killing our fellow co-workers, but if we don't, it could be the last moments we see ourselves alive," he finished as he closed in on the toolshed only moments from the mess hall.

They all followed behind into the shed. Rook stepped away from O'Malley, and then gestured he was okay to move about on his own. Hank made his way to the back, and smiled when he grabbed his choice of weapon, with his strength, a chainsaw was an obvious choice. "Well, if the trees are alive and moving, I'll definitely have no problem."

Rook couldn't carry anything too heavy, so he moved along the wall—holding himself up—browsing the single-handed tools. "This should do," he grunted, showing strength in holding back the pain; the meds helped. He took hold of a sickle used mostly for tall grass.

When Rook made his way away from O'Malley, he too searched for his weapon of choice. He needed defense so he could defend the evidence he procured. "This laptop could be the only thing that could convince the authorities," he often thought. The government could cover everything up, but they couldn't deny the actual documentation. O'Malley thought range would be best, so he took hold of a hay fork often used to carry the chopped grass and weeds from the site to be burned or turned into mulch. "Nice," was all he uttered in approval of his choice.

Aaliyah wasn't all too certain what to use. The anxiety she sheltered in her mind started to calm now, being that she felt safe now that they were armed. But all that changed when she saw it; it was a hedge trimmer hiding just out of eyeshot peeking out from behind the shed door. Her unease turned to utter confidence when she realized she now was pretty secure.

"Okay, is everyone ready?" Hank uttered once he realized everyone was 'packing.' They all acknowledged him with either a verbal response or a nod. "Good, now let's kick this God-forsaken-weird-phenomenon's ass, and get the bastard responsible for this shit!" The random pep talk sparked a fire in everyone there, even distracting Rook from his pain for the moment, and with that, he led the group onward.

The eerie nature of the woods continued as if the very wind held a damning call upon itself. It carried the faint screams and gasps of air through the sound of gurgling of blood as if the woods echoed the pain of the death it harvested. It brought chills to the whole group as they pressed forward, clenching onto the weapons they wielded. At this hour, the sky still wasn't sure what time of day it was, but it continued to resemble the blackest of nights.

At this moment, it occurred to at least one that if the lights worked earlier along with the walkies and the laptop, that possibly her cell phone could work, too. Aaliyah held her trimmer to her side for a moment to rummage into her pockets for her cellular device, and the action made the others stop as well. "Guys?! When was the last time you checked your cell phones for a signal?"

They were shocked that none had even thought of it because of all that was happening in correlation to the ominous sky. "Well, ain't that something," O'Malley too pulled out his phone to check.

They actually powered up. "Mine's actually starting!"

"Mine as well!" O'Malley was shocked.

Hank didn't even bother to look; he didn't have one. It explains why it didn't even cross his mind, "Fine, but hurry. The light could attract someone or something." He wasn't wrong. The lights shone bright through the darkness, cutting around the trees.

Then in an instant, the phones started to glitch before their very eyes. Plaid and broken data gave way to static as a figure shown on both screens simultaneously. Rook didn't even bother with his phone at this point; the pain to reach into his own pants was excruciating. "What the fuck," was either spoken between a few of them or was at least shown across their faces. Then what shone on the screen uncurled their hair as it rose in goosebumps, River shone through the static as a living, breathing entity.

"Help me! Why did you just leave me hanging, girl?! I'm still alive. Aaliyah, baby!" He spoke as if it were really him. She was in tears by now. She saw this as redemption as for whatever this was tore at her already fragile psyche.

"Don't believe what he's saying," Rook grunted through his teeth, but his wound was starting to be even harder to handle, leaving him too quiet to break through Aaliyah's current delusion.

"So wait, is River alive?" O'Malley spoke poorly, even getting thrown off himself, and it was just enough to cause Aaliyah to fling herself toward where River's body was, dropping her form of defense in the process, the trimmer.

"No!" Hank tore through the group to catch up to Aaliyah, but she had more youthful vigor than that of him.

Tears tore off her face as twigs and leaves were crushed beneath her feet until—

THUMP

She crashed into something—or someone. Her near exhaustion gave way to a rising fear as whatever it was wrapped its grip around her instantly cradling her impact. Then as she started to look up, it spoke. "I knew you still cared, babe." It sounded like River, and the sheer voice pierced violently in her stomach causing the feeling of pure dread to hit her like a swift hook to the gut. She trembled in fear as her eyes finally met her captor's gaze. It was River, but his appearance was revolting.

His black skin was corroded in a base of green that looked to have originated in his veins. The green sprouted into vines that wrapped its way up around the whole body finishing towards the top of the head laying like a crown of branches around the hair, only one of River's eyes was uncovered. Right after he spoke, he began to undergo a terrifying transformation. As he held tightly now to Aaliyah, and her struggling having no effect on his grip, he tore his neck from the base, lifting his head to tower over the rest of himself. The vines made it so with swiftness, and the bloodcurdling sounds of broken bones. His jaw widened in the same manner as the skin tearing itself to enlarge the mouth. Green sludge spurted out onto her face as his head swung around before lunging down to savagely decapitate her with a massive bite.

But Hank closed the gap in time! He took the attack straight to the shoulder as he pushed Aaliyah out the way with enough force to free her. She struck the ground as he yelled in immense pain. Blood spilled on all close enough as it rained. The sight made O'Malley's legs buckle and collapse leaving him shocked, and on the ground.

As Aaliyah screamed at the sheer horror that befell Hank, Rook swung his sickle with precision, nearly cutting through the monster's neck. Green gushed out, and now the hysteric creature in desperation dropped Hank, and slammed Rook causing him to fly even further than where O'Malley sat shocked in place. He hit hard, and now laid out cold.

Now River's eye lay defenseless, and Aaliyah sat weeping in terror before him. She hurried back, kicking wildly at its head that crept closer to her as she tried to quickly stand. She managed to get to her feet and started to run in the opposite direction. Then the monster lunged at her, and in that moment, Hank stuck his chainsaw deep into the wounded neck. Pinning it down, he quickly pulled the cord, starting it up shredding its neck, dealing massive damage.

River's scream pierced their ears with horrible unease as its neck gushed green goop everywhere like a broken spout. Its neck now lay severed from the body only inches from where Aaliyah was standing. She burst into tears instantly, and ran straight into her hero's arms. "You're bleeding! We need to patch that up."

"Yeah, that's probably what I'll do," Hank said back with a weak chuckle. Then he collapsed. He lost too much blood.

"Hank!" Her tears were distracted by his sudden collapse. His adrenaline kept him up, but now he clung to life.

At that moment, O'Malley flung himself down next to him, and he then ripped his shirt open, and applied pressure to the wound. "Aaliyah! I'm going to need you to put pressure on the wound. I managed to bring the med kit inside the laptop bag, but I'm not sure it'll be enough."

Aaliyah took hold of the rag and held pressure so that he could rummage in the laptop bag. He pulled out some alcohol with clean cloth, medical tape, and butterfly stitches. "Okay, pull away, and I'm going to quickly toss some alcohol on the wound to keep it from getting infected. Then I'm going to need you to wipe the wounds with a clean cloth, and try to keep it clean as I apply the stitches. Last, we'll apply the medical tape to better hold the stitches, and hold back the blood so he doesn't bleed out." He walked her through the process.

Her shocked look turned to relief. Hank was stable, but unconscious. Rook was another story though. "Okay, mate, you're next." O'Malley quickly attended to Rook's wounds as Aaliyah comforted Hank. "I'm going to need to remove these band—" He halted his words in shock when Rook groaned at him for removing his bandages because Rook's wound was massively infected. What happened to River was slowly, but surely, coursing through his veins as well. "Oh fuck?!" O'Malley regretted saying this as it didn't put Rook at ease.

"So I'm guessing it's bad." Rook grinded his teeth trying to formulate words.

The wound was dark from the dried blood, but it also held shades of green as it expanded across his body bulging out his veins in a grotesque manner. He was definitely going to die. The shape he was in caused him to sweat profusely. He would clench his teeth in pain because the pain was too unbearable to move. He was shaking as well, showing signs of a fever.

"Yeah, mate, it's pretty bad, but at least now we can say you got some color." O'Malley chuckled.

"You're an ass." Rook painfully laughed coughing afterwards. "Of course you'd joke during a time like this. That's always what I liked about you, man." At this point, Aaliyah now stood over them, tearing up. She was about to lose another friend, and he noticed her and said, "No need to cry. I'm just happy I got to spend what remaining time I had with you guys. Now get going. You still have some answers to get from those fuckers." He struggled to laugh.

"Bite your tongue. We'll still make it together. That scientist has got to have an antidote." O'Malley shined false hope in Rook's way.

He hushed O'Malley. "You know that's not true. There is no hope you'd be able to make it back to me in time."

While they talked, Aaliyah looked back and forth between the wounded, looking out for them and their surroundings. Then a rustle from the bushes that leered only a couple feet away caught her attention. Dread burrowed into her chest as anxiety gave way to paranoia. "Guys, there is something out there."

She reached for the nearest weapon that lay at her side, the chainsaw that Hank used to sever River's neck from his body. She began to pull the cord with desperation, and O'Malley did the same with the trimmer to defend Rook's last waking moments. Then what lunged out from the leafy darkness as the motors hummed from the companions' arsenal was the last person they thought would come for them, Mark.

He actually looked badly wounded, covered in blood. Then Mark spoke as he tried to lift himself from the ground. "They are coming."

Aaliyah grew frightened. "Wait! Who's coming?"

O'Malley just stood on guard. "And where the fuck you been?! And why the Hell should we even trust you?"

Mark finally got back to his feet. "Because I may be your only chance to survive this Hell."

How could anyone trust this bastard after the evidence they saw?

O'Malley guarded said evidence that sat beside Rook. Rook's last moments ticked away as their attention solely remained trained on Mark. "I don't give a fuck! You better explain yourself, you cocksucker!" He held no anger back, and for good reasons.

"You don't understand. We have to get out of here first!" Mark seemed rather desperate as he currently stood gripping his wounds in pain. Then more rustling began to surface from other bushes in the vicinity. "Ah shit, they're already here."

"What's here?!" Aaliyah questioned again.

"The remaining workers," he answered quickly as they started to emerge.

"We need to go now!" O'Malley stated as they started to get ready for a sprint.

"What about the others? We can't just leave—" Before Aaliyah could finish what she was desperately saying, Rook stood up, pushing through the pain.

"I've got this. Just take Hank and go." Rook didn't sound full of strength, but rather he sounded nearly departed as his voice faded off toward the end. He stood ready to fight with what strength he had with his sickle in hand. O'Malley and Aaliyah felt conflicted as they both lifted up Hank and headed off.

"Follow me, I know of a safe haven out in these woods not far off from here," said Mark quickly as he passed by them to lead the way.

"I guess we have no choice at this point," Aaliyah whispered to O'Malley.

"This could be our chance for answers," he whispered back as they followed Mark.

Rook stood ready for battle as his face showed pure agony. His veins pierced his body like hellfire as his time waned. His legs buckled as the creatures screeched toward him. They all resembled that of what River became, and he knew he'd also end up the same. He swung his sickle toward the first that came close. He clipped it enough to push it away, but the next, with a massive crunch, tore his left arm clean off. Rook took his last breath as the rest of the monsters ate at his flesh.

The others got far away enough where they could still hear Rook's blood-curdling scream but were still out of the creatures' line of sight. Aaliyah shed a single tear as she held back further ones. "We have to keep moving. Can't slow up now," Mark urged the grieving so they could get to the safehouse he had mentioned moments ago.

As they continued, O'Malley had to ask, "Where are we going?"

"Where you'll find answers that I know you desperately seek. The scientist's refuge. He has a cabin not much further from here," Mark answered with the remark that would best satisfy O'Malley and Aaliyah the most with a short and quick reply without coercion. They aren't keen to follow him, but this was definitely what needed to be done.

"Fine," O'Malley didn't need to say much as he wore a look of distrust for him on his face. Because they had to carry Hank to safety, they also needed to recover, or they wouldn't be able to survive the rest of the night.

They arrived at the cabin as rustling trailed behind them. The creatures scoured the darkness as they entered the cabin, and they bolted the door behind them. The cabin was immensely dark, and it needed to be to hide the group from a very plausible death. They worked out a plan on the way in. "Okay, close shutters on the windows, and if you need any light to see, use your phone if you have battery life. Make sure you turn it down low, we needn't attract those monsters out there," Mark commanded, instantly trying to take charge.

"Who the fuck made you captain, traitor?!" O'Malley straight away debated against Mark's right to lead.

"Just want to make sure you live long enough to be able to hear my defense from your false accusations," Mark retorted, and then continued. "Now listen, I'm not just an ordinary lumber worker like you two. I was actually brought in to investigate a potential bioweapon and terrorist attack that'd be seen as an attack on our nation. It's currently limited to this area, but we are led to believe that Doctor Daniel Avery Gluberman is the cause of this viral outbreak."

"Wait?! So this means he's not creating a potential cure, but rather spreading the infection?" Aaliyah jumped in. "I'm... just—I'm going to need a moment... I—I'll go take a look around." She wasn't ready to have all hopes dashed, so she decided to get her mind off the current dilemma by distracting herself with the potential clues lying about the cabin.

O'Malley began again, "So we're infected by a possible prototype bio-weapon with no possible cure, and you're a part of a government agency that investigates bioterrorism?"

"Yes, and that's all I can disclose, but at this current moment, there is no guarantee we'll get out of this alive. But I can at least ask for your help in making sure this virus doesn't spread." Mark looked desperate enough in his current state. O'Malley had severe trust issues toward him, and didn't plan on releasing the evidence on his person. "Wait, is that my laptop with you?"

"Don't even think about it. I'm not sure I believe you enough to hand over the only bit of evidence I have on what's going on here." O'Malley held the laptop around his back, protecting it from his grasp. "If you lead us to the scientist, and put an end to this madness, I'll consider handing your laptop back."

"You think I'm capable of handling this alone?! My men are on the outside. I'm alone on this, and I'm begging for your help. If we do not do it for me, then do it for the rest of America. If this spreads, we could be damning the whole Goddamn country," Mark spouted compassion in his tone.

While he sat on the couch contemplating, Hank lay unconscious still beside him. Aaliyah started looking around first in the hallway that connected the living room of the cabin to the kitchen. While they talked in the distance, she came across a photo that lay face down on a cabinet. She picked it up to see a picture of a scientist and his assistant, but the assistant's face was scratched out, violently attacked.

She didn't plan to reveal this information yet. She pushed even further with her phone as a source of light on the lowest setting toward the kitchen. The place smelled awful as food that lay sprawled across the table was molded. It seems the scientist wasn't here, and hadn't been for awhile. So did that mean he was dead? "He mustn't have visited this cabin for quite some time," she thought to herself, "and why would he have a cabin out here in the first place? This must have all been premeditated."

She continued her search while the guys' conversation concluded. "Fine, I wasn't planning on revealing this, but if we don't end this soon, then Hell will rain down on us in the form of an airstrike. Yes, that means to make sure this doesn't spread anymore, we'll be bombing the woods." Mark started to get heated, and got quiet by the end of his statement.

O'Malley's face showed a look of fearful anger, "So that's the solution to everything in America, just blow the fucking shite out of everything?" It was a rhetorical question.

"That's why we need to end this before we resort to drastic measures," Mark emphasized with hand gestures after breathing heavily behind his hands.

"Fine, what do you need us to do?" He gave into his whim, but trust was far from the reason.

Aaliyah entered back into the front room as the conversation came to a close. "Hey, I don't think we're going to find the doctor around here. It doesn't look like he has been here for days."

"Based on the knowledge I acquired in my early surveillance, the doctor was only here for the earlier stages. We are grasping at straws when coming here in the first place," Mark explained.

Aaliyah looked as bummed as O'Malley looked after hearing all that. "So then where would he be?" She had to ask.

"I'd say he embedded himself deep inside the woods toward the center. He'd need control of the mass, so he'd probably position himself near the oldest tree in the woods." Mark seemed to have planned this out almost too well. "I'm going to need my laptop now. It'll help me pinpoint the longitude and latitude of where this bastard is. Please, you have to trust me. This is our only shot. The longer we wait, the faster this virus deteriorates your body. We don't have much longer."

O'Malley's face scrunched up as he contemplated his choices, and he realized that he was very convincing. "Fine! Here, take it. I know this is the only way." Mark nodded as O'Malley handed over the laptop bag.

"Thanks, you won't regret it." Mark smiled, but O'Malley wasn't so sure.

Aaliyah awaited the plan to be active as she took a wet rag to Hank's forehead. She felt indebted to him, and she was going to see this to the end for him. The moist sensation woke Hank from his sleep. "Where am I?"

She was quick to comfort him. "Somewhere safe, just rest for now."

"Thank you." He smiled.

"No, it's me who should be thanking you." She kind of blushed, and hastily spoke.

"You're so modest, but I'm thanking you for more than saving me, and helping me to safety," he grunted in pain, and took a breath as he sat himself up. "I'm also thanking you for being by my side. I might not get another chance to say this because of all this shit, but… I love you, Aaliyah."

She definitely blushed. She was speechless. She knew their feelings were mutual, but they only kept themselves in a stage of flirting. It was more now. She threw herself into him on an impulse of butterflies. He groaned. "I'm sorry," she said, and quickly backed off.

"No, no, It's fine. I'm just so happy now. I can fight through the pain." He gave a weary smile, and it made her smile, too.

"Okay, the plan is set. I know where the doctor should be," Mark exclaimed. "We should survey our surroundings, and see if it's okay to leave. The more time we waste, the quicker we die."

"I can't argue with that," Hank groaned on his way up from his seat.

"You shouldn't move so fast. You might pull your stitches," Aaliyah jumped in.

"Thanks." Hank showed praise.

"Yeah, we have no choice. It's now or never." O'Malley stood and walked to the window. "I'm not seeing any movement out there."

"Well, that means it's time to move out." Mark took command again, placed his laptop back in the bag, and draped it over his shoulder. He looked to make sure O'Malley didn't get his hands on it again. "We shouldn't linger here, but it wouldn't be safe going out there without protection. Gather some weapons before we leave. We have to make sure we at least survive until we reach the doctor." He made a good point as he directed them to the kitchen.

He was implying using knives from the kitchen. O'Malley didn't trust him at all, so he felt Mark was hiding something involving this location like was this even the doctor's place, or perhaps was this actually someone else's. As Mark walked them in toward the kitchen, he gently placed the photo that stood on the cabinets back down after Aaliyah had left it there earlier. Why would he care?

Before he had done that with the photo, O'Malley got a glimpse of the photo, and now he knew nearly as much as Aaliyah did at this moment. He wasn't about to ask him what that was about, but when the moment came, they would break away from him. "Okay, is everybody ready to head out?" Mark asked as he stood in the center of the archway of the stairs that lead up.

Now he blocked the upstairs. "What gives?" O'Malley thought. He gave Aaliyah a look, and she did so back. He was acting fishy.

"Yeah, I'm ready," Hank said as he was the last to arm himself. He was too concerned with his own preservation to be interested in Mark, but he wasn't far off from thinking the same way as the other two.

"We don't have much time. The way is clear. We'll go out the back door. I memorized the route we're taking. Now pile out," Mark instructed as he looked through the blinds of the back window. They did so. Mark followed behind, then made his way to the front of the line. Aaliyah had her back turned to him, but perhaps he didn't realize she had. O'Malley noticed first, and then Hank seconds later; she was hiding something she found in the house earlier. It was a gun tucked behind her back.

She nodded toward them, but they didn't acknowledge for long not to bring suspicion to the table. Mark didn't need to be warned by their distrust, but they had a feeling he already knew. Anxiety swelled up in all of them. The guys pushed in front of Aaliyah to move as cover. Their hearts felt like they were going to burst with agony towards the potential danger that loomed.

"Come on. We are nearly there." Mark broke the silence as he further distanced himself by moving further ahead. What was the meaning of that? It only filled them with more unease.

They hustled on toward where he ran off to, but he was nowhere to be found. So they cautiously continued on, and Hank put one finger in front of his mouth, signaling them to keep it down as voices started to grow louder in the distance. It was Mark, and it sounded like he had an intensity in his voice, one of resentments. "How could you do this to all these people? I should put you down where you stand."

They took to the shadows as they listened in on the conversation that burst through the trees. Mark had Dr. Gluberman at gunpoint. When did he get a gun, or did he always have one? They stood in front of a massive tree that glowed with a blue intensity that had vines hanging from the top base that felt dangerous as if they excreted fear. It felt as if the air density was heavier the closer to the tree they got, and at the base of the tree trunk laid a flora spectacle. Gray and purple flowers littered the ground as if the ground looked scorched with a shade of violet, the flora looked to be evolving.

The scene illuminated by the tree foreshadowed an uneasy feeling as dread started to swell in the depths of their souls; something was coming. The group was hidden well, and they noticed the others of the work site, now mutated, starting to case the area. They stopped inches from the clearing, and stood in the shadows. "You're outnumbered Mark," the doctor spoke as his raised hands started to fall.

"Wait, he knew his name. He is the assistant." Aaliyah was mildly shocked as a flashback to the photo she saw moments ago brought the pieces together. He must have been the one who actually lived in that cabin prior to joining the workforce, but what was his game?

"That fucking bastard." O'Malley came to realize it as well.

"I know you didn't bring that gun to recollect fond memories with your old mentor now, but if you were planning to kill me, you should have already shot me." Dr. Gluberman, in a blink of an eye, was wrapped in a cocoon as Mark pulled the trigger, but the rounds couldn't pierce the thick bark of the roots. The roots entangled themselves around the doctor until what was left to be seen of the doctor wasn't visible at all.

"He is distracted! This would be a good time now, Aaliyah."

O'Malley pointed to the gun. Seeing how Mark was connected to the scientist didn't fill in all the questions; there was still something they weren't seeing.

But before she could act, Hank spoke with clear confidence, "Give me the gun. After seeing what happened to Rook, I'd say I don't have much time left as well. I'll end this so you won't have to."

Aaliyah spoke quickly, and with a hint of shatter to her soul, "You can't." She was shaking with tears starting to swell, but she wasn't willing to lose him just yet.

"Please." He started to reach for the gun, but she yanked the gun away with a stern look on her face, and tears in her eyes. After everything, he knew that those weren't tears of melancholy, but rather they were of hatred. She then darted out of the hiding place towards Mark, and now she held Mark at gunpoint.

"Oh, there you guys are. I thought we had a plan—"

"Save it!" She screamed at him with clenched teeth. "We know you're working with this bastard, and I'm going to make your last moments painful. Did none of us even matter to you?"

He started to laugh, holding it back the best he could. "Okay, you got me. I had to spin a story for you guys so I could get to here unharmed, but now it seems I've lost." He turned around slowly, and held his hands up.

"Toss the gun, now!" Her grip on the gun tightened while her friends awaited in awe in the shadows.

"Not a smart decision, but fine." He tossed it. "Any moment now, that scientist you feared will wake from his cocooned slumber, and according to my research you're going to need the firepower."

After he finished, the cocoon pulsated, and that moment was enough to distract Aaliyah's focus from him just enough so he could rush her, pinning her to the ground, causing the gun to miss when she fired. The gun zoomed off into the distance. That's when O'Malley and Hank charged in.

"Still trying to control everything, huh, Mark?" A monstrous being unsheathed itself from the cocoon, and Aaliyah's heart dropped as dread and fear became overbearing. Sheer terror gave her the strength to fight back as it led to a pistol whip to his face. In that moment, Hank mustered up a swift kick to Mark's face as O'Malley pulled Aaliyah out from underneath him.

Mark just burst out laughing which only tightened the grip of uneasiness in the air surrounding the scene. "Why are you laughing? Don't you know you've lost?" said the horrid monster that floated high above him with a booming and gruff voice as if his lungs were being constricted by the very vines that lifted him up. His body was now bark and green as if he were more tree than man, covered in moss. His veins illuminated neon green through his hardened skin, but it seemed as though the crevices leaked like the goo from the creatures in the woods surrounding.

Something was off...

Then the creature that towered before them dropped as the goo seeped from the mouth now; it coughed profusely. "What's happening to me?" It spoke in bewilderment, and in pain as it collapsed. It was dying.

Mark started to maniacally laugh even harder. "Because, you foolish old man, it's rejecting your DNA. Do you think I would trudge my way through this project not to come on top?"

The dying creature in desperation lunged a root that shot from its palm toward him, but Mark only turned his head and stared at the attempt to stop him with a smirk. That was the moment that Aaliyah, Hank, and O'Malley came to the conclusion they were duped the whole time. He was never hurt, and he never worked alongside them. He weaseled his way under the radar with deception, and a trick of the eye.

Mark's eyes glowed blue in unison to the vines that hung from the massive tree, and the flowers underneath bloomed, releasing spores that twinkled across the opening. "This is the end game, old man. You never were in charge of this program. I was! I embedded my DNA into the mutation, and you had no clue. I resented you! You thought you were so smart, but I clearly was more crafty!"

As Mark ranted on, Aaliyah and Hank slowly started towards the firearms that laid on the cold ground right in front of them. Mark was clearly an egomaniac preoccupied with his revenge. As he moved closer to Dr. Gluberman, his appearance came all too clear as his skin started to mimic that of his mentor. "Well, I guess this is goodbye," he whispered into his ear as he kneeled down beside his dying mentor. A root then penetrated the chest of Dr. Gluberman as he choked on his own sap.

In that moment, the party took their chances at salvation, and they unloaded what lead they had into Mark's back, not knowing that the flora surrounding their feet was hindering them. Dizziness came like a spell, and their eyes felt swimmy as the world just spun. Hank went down, instantly succumbing first to the unbalance because of his injuries. Aaliyah stood strong as O'Malley began to vomit from the vertigo. He then succumbed next.

"What the fuck?! I can't even stand," Hank spoke loudly as he tried to stand on his feet with a tremble, to no prevail.

Aaliyah gradually trudged with each step, easing herself closer to Mark. "Awe, can you still stand? That's cute," Mark said mockingly.

"Fuck... off," she told him, trying to fight the vertigo.

"You definitely are of the superior breed, but I'll show them that I'm what they want... With your end," he finished as he controlled the roots below his feet to lift him up. He began his metamorphosis, but Aaliyah was having none of it. She jumped on the roots, and rode them up with Mark as he held his arms out like some sort of crucifixion like he was some chosen God.

"No... Don't!" Hank tried to yell, but he nearly gagged up his breakfast from the strain.

She started to climb as she pulled out the blade she acquired from the cabin moments ago. The vertigo dwindled as her focus persevered. She continued up as the blue illuminated vines started to work their way towards Mark as he started to wrap himself in a cocoon just like his ex-mentor before him, but he aspired to finish the process, being he was the catalyst to begin with.

The vines pumped their essence into the cocoon, illuminating the area in a glow. Hank and O'Malley had no choice but to bask in the glow, and

Aaliyah struggled to position herself alongside the pulsating cocoon, holding on with all her might as she donned her knife. She began with a quip. "I hope you enjoy this prick!" And she then struck her blade swiftly into one of the vines. It violently trembled as its innards spewed out.

The vine she struck violently twirled as if it were in pain. The blue now covered her as she went for another one. Trying to see so she could adjust herself was a struggle, and the fear started to swell greatly alongside her exhaustion for her grip became harder to hold. The shock to the cocoon caused its pulsations to quicken as if it were a heart having a panic attack, and that all resulted in an evident countdown. Knowing that the hive mind was in trouble, the horrid creatures surrounding the area then reacted to the horror, and charged toward her efforts.

She noticed but had no time to concern herself, but the terror of the thought rose with dread in her heart, causing unneeded butterflies in the pit of her stomach. She sliced another vine, and nearly lost her grip in the process. Her heart raced, but she couldn't quit now because she had the creatures below that would tear her apart. They started to climb the stalk, inching closer and closer to her rapidly. She hastened her assault on the entity, but her fear attacked her continuity and she grew hesitant. She persevered through.

Hank and O'Malley began their assault on the ground trying to hold off what creatures they could, but to their surprise, they didn't acknowledge them because the threat was striking desperately uptop the stalk. With repetition, they thrust their blades into the creatures as they tried to climb, causing more sap to spew on the ground. Creatures dropped one by one, but it wasn't enough to keep them all from Aaliyah, especially since both Hank and O'Malley were hindered, if not by wounds then by vertigo.

Aaliyah neared completion as she started to suffer from fatigue. Her arms became strenuous, and her muscles began to spasm. The creatures now clawed at her heels. She groaned, "Fuck off!" She felt piercing pain as the claws dug into her legs. She desperately kicked them away, knocking some, but not all, back down as those landed on top of others.

"Oy, watch it!" O'Malley beckoned as one almost landed on him.

"Almost," Aaliyah encouraged herself as she gripped the last vine. Before she could finish off the last vine, some of the monsters managed to climb beside her. They swiftly started to attack her in a frenzy. She struck them either at the hands or the head, suffering from their blows in the process.

She then theorized her focus, at possibly the cost of her life, should be solely on the last vine. So suffering a blow to her side, claws dug into her as she screamed in pain causing a moment that allowed her to slit right through the last appendage. The cocoon compulsively wagged, trying to shake off what was on it. Its pulsations looked to resemble that of lungs that gasped for breath.

Aaliyah held on for dear life as the other creatures now plummeted to the Earth's surface. In that moment of blurry dismay from the blood loss, she was then caught off guard by the shock of the cocoon opening up. She nearly slipped as she jumped from the scare. It was Mark within the final stages of his metamorphosis; he was gasping for air because what fed him was what he needed was sabotaged by her. She peered into his black eyes, seeing his dark soul asking desperately for release. He was dying.

Then in a fell swoop with the last of her energy, she stuck him right in the eye avoiding the decaying bark across his face. His presence held no light within him. The blue glow rested on her, and not in him. "It's… over," were the last words she uttered before her energy reserves ran out. What was left in the creature seeped the remaining life-force, and rained like waterfalls out of its body.

As she fell after letting go of the blade, she felt accomplished, the evil entity started to harden, and wither away like a log caught a blaze. In a slow state, the nightmare faded as her eyes began to close. The skies began to clear, the creatures withered, too, alongside the hive mind, and her friends that remained were alive in the end. One tear left her eye as she slammed into the ground.

Black

Not even minutes later, the vertigo wore off, and Hank stumbled across the decrepit field of now withered flowers that was haunted by the mausoleum of corpses that resembled a scorched battlefield whose flames had died out hours ago. Ashes fluttered like snow in the breeze. He collapsed at Aaliyah's side. She wasn't exactly dead, the complete opposite actually. "What the fuck?" he said as he noticed the blue goop seeping inside her wounds, miraculously healing her injuries before him. "Awe, shit." He gripped his shoulder realizing his wounds had reopened. He realized he didn't have much time left as is, but O'Malley creeped up on him, and he hoped he could help. "Thank God... You're okay, friend." He had a troubling sound in his voice.

"Don't worry, I got you," said O'Malley in an unfamiliar tone.

"Wait... what happened to—" In that instant, Hank's words were halted by the blade that violently stabbed into his neck. His eyes faded into a milky white still retaining the shock of betrayal from O'Malley.

"The subject is secure, and the loose ends are taken care of. Moving into position for rendezvous." He dropped his phony accent for his true American one as he spoke into a walkie that now would work because interference by the strange phenomenon wasn't a problem now. He then casually walked from the pool of blood of his comrade toward the edge of the forest-line, pulling a laptop out from within one of the burrows at the base of a tree. "I have secured the research, now awaiting extraction."

The sound of a CH-47F Chinook helicopter approached the clearing carrying in suspension underneath a massive titanium casing containment pod. It gently set the pod down feet away from Aaliyah's unconscious body, crushing the remains of some of the ashened victims. Then it gently landed on the other side of the clearing doing the same damage to the ashened as soldiers poured out fully decked out in an arsenal of equipment, even including AK's and gasmasks.

"Clear," one of the soldiers spoke as they approached Aaliyah, who was still laying there unaware.

Behind them, a scientist hopped out from the chopper tailing the soldiers. "Remarkable, it seems Dr. Gluberman's research was promising after all," he continued as he knelt beside her, and picked up her arm, "I see the mutation is beginning to take effect. Carry on," he commanded as he walked back to the chopper. The soldiers carried the poor girl to the pod securing her in except one soldier, who seemed to be more distinguished than the others, walked toward O'Malley.

"Good work, soldier. I'll make sure you get a medal for serving your country, son," He patted his shoulder with his one free arm as the other held his firearm.

"Thank you, Sir." He saluted his superior, then followed him onto the chopper for takeoff.

"Here you go. You're going to need this." His superior handed him what looked like a badge that read his rank and real name, 'Lt. Arnold Rager.'

EPILOGUE

In the darkness, she felt cold. Where was she? She awoke feeling great, completely refreshed. She felt new as her vision started to peel away in the dark. Her eyes now possessed a blue hue to them. She could see in the dark. It amazed her, but this all broke to a terrifying reality. She was shackled to a cold titanium prison. She started to panic, hyperventilate even. She screamed and screamed—and screamed, but no one would hear her screams. Aaliyah was helpless to her captors' whims. She just cried, "Help," over and over again, but she halted her failed attempts when she realized her body now looked hardened like bark. This only made her cry even harder, even sobbing. All was hopeless.

• • •

Down in the clearing, something struggled to live, something miniature pushed itself from the ashes that littered the base of the withered tree that once almost made a monstrous God of Gluberman, and then Mark. It looked grotesque as it crawled out from the pile it was in like a phoenix rebirthed from its ashes. It was a fleshy acorn that sprouted arachnid-like limbs to grasp onto life. It scuttled to the nearest fleshy remains near it, Hank.

It halted for a moment when it reached the head of this departed hero before making its way past the knife that lay embedded into his neck, and on to his mouth. It forced itself into the recesses of his mouth pushing past the oral cavity of his throat, and on its way to the heart. It nestled in the heart jumpstarting the remains. The body was alive again, and it opened its eyes suddenly as it gasped for carbon dioxide. The wounds began to heal miraculously like Aaliyah's. The knife in the throat then was pushed out as the hole closed up behind it.

This reanimated corpse spoke right after a maniacal laughter, "Not the body I was hoping for, but it'll do." It then stood up, groaning, "Also stiffer than expected, but still that bitch doesn't have a chance in Hell." Its eyes gleamed with a hull of blue as it left the clearing.

• • •

In a classified location deep underground in a facility somewhere within Washington, DC, massive monitors illuminated mechanical controls and computers being used by scientists guarded by American armed forces. These scientists were monitoring their new test subject deemed 'Project Sapphire.' On the screen were detailed reports of the undercover expedition piloted by Lt. Arnold Rager.

Faces sprung up on the screens of the failed and accomplished subjects: Bethany, Hank, Aaliyah, River, Mark, and Dr. Gluberman. Red 'X's' crossed off through Bethany's, Hank's, Mark's, River's, and Glumberman's faces as being listed as deceased and as failed experiments, but one face then shone across the screens listed with tests already enacted on her.

Bethany was listed as 'incompatible blood' which resulted in early hallucinations. Hank was listed as too 'resilient' to the mutation. River was listed as 'mentally incapable' of bonding. Mark was listed as 'uncontrollable' and had to be terminated—as if they expected it. Gluberman was listed as 'incompetent' and had to also be terminated, but Aaliyah showed promise, and was listed as 'adaptable' and as compatible for further testing. "If we can find how the mutation embedded itself inside 'Project Sapphire,' then we have a chance at making our forces nearly invincible; if not, practically immortal," a scientist with a clipboard spoke to a high ranking general.

"Good, at this pace, our country will be officially the most powerful nation for generations to come. There will be no threat that can threaten our borders like ISIS or the Russians ever again. Good work, keep me up to date when we finally discover the chemical bond needed to create super soldiers. No longer will families have to lose their loved ones for American progression for global freedom, carry on doctor," finished the general with his monologue, and after he walked out leaving the scientist to his nerves, nodded in agreement.

The last thing that shone on the screen before being taken off the monitor was a sedated Aaliyah laying strapped to a gurney as scientists continued to prod at her. The horror was gruesome, but it continued to provide one fact: she was no longer human.

The Supernatural Inclinations of a Deli Culinarian: Soul Swallowing Void

I have no recollection of how long I've been here, but someone needs to exist to craft the food presented to the souls that roam in this dimension. Nothing looks savory, but something or someone comes to devour sooner or later. Who's to say when anything needs to be changed out as well, sooner or later it's just gone, and that's when I cook the monstrous concoctions.

After many existences, I've not aged. I just carry bags that way down my eyes, and raven black hair that no longer shines. As I stare into the void of the fryer, I see my eyes are a milky blue like I've lost my soul years ago. Am I even to know if I had a gender once upon a time? My image fluctuates between female and male genitals, depending on the souls that walk to the counter. They see what they see, and even though I seem vacant, I still carry a sense of beauty being male, female, or other.

I need to welcome the guests, and this void believes the guide must be that of beauty it seems. As I prepare the next batch of horrors, a fragile old man walks from the nothingness that swallows the rest of the surroundings besides the random existing deli, or is it necessary that this deli exist? As I approach the counter, my hair shortens and I grow appendages on my chest, and the old man's eyes widen in shock.

"Lisa?" he muttered as he trembled due to Parkinson's.

It seems he sees a resemblance of his daughter before him, but even I'm not sure of what this void acquires from this change, and I just continue my work like I've done so many times before. "Welcome, how may I assist you?"

The man calmed rather strangely, in fact like others before him, it's the void. This domain's calming effect carries all around like a lure to bait. And in that moment, he only uttered one word, "hunger."

"What are you hungry for, Sir?" I started to wear a wicked smile because this was the moment that made my existence worth living, the instant of just dues.

"I... I... I hunger for young girls." He started to tremble again when he realized what he said. This place carried in its space something that worked like a truth agent, not exactly air but a mist that's quite similar.

The man sobbed uncontrollably, now drenching his suit he wore by wiping his tears with his cuffs. "I have just the meal, sir." I walked to the fryer seeing it was now finished, not remembering exactly when I started cooking. I lifted the fryer net from the blackened grease that boiled intensely. As expected, something was attached to the net, bidding me to say hello. A childlike arm rose from the black with the net, but now letting go as I pulled it free from the bubbling cesspool. The hand fell back in as I gave it a smile. It looked to be a heart it carried in the net, still beating.

I lifted the heart in my hand as the blood still oozed out on my hand. I placed it in a carrier, and priced it accordingly. "The price, sir, comes to an eternity of damnation."

He only continued to break down as he accepted the container, and opened it before me, and began to munch vigorously like he had no choice. My wicked grin returned, why I come to enjoy these moments I don't know, but perhaps maybe they are my only joy.

He now no longer held the appearance of an old man, but that of a little girl. Blood covered his gown, a pretty pink dress which was complemented with short pigtails, and from the nothingness came another old man whose eyes were darkened with malice. He didn't tremble. He only smiled as he escorted the little girl away into the black, and I turned to work again on making the next batch of horrors.

Creak

I succumb to this lifestyle-this destiny, a purpose only I can fulfill. I exist, but don't feel alive nor human at this point. Life is to live, and I only survive. I'm trapped here with this entity—this monster. I watch her with content, but also with disdain. I hate her, a rippling echo of what was once my wife. I lost track of the days, weeks, months, or perhaps years. I yearn for freedom, but I also yearn for existing captivity. The torment tears at my soul.

I distract myself on a daily basis.

Click, Clack

…On the keyboard as I type away my life story. The daughter I miss and the love I yearn for creep within eyeshot of my peripheral vision. Their visage is of pain and agony as I don't stare, but rather I listen with fear and disgust as she lingers in the darkness of the other room. The horror would intensify the moment her presence would be known.

Creeeeaaakk

The door opening is the greatest fear I've known until this day, because it meant she was here once again. I could scream—I could resort to violence, but I can't bring myself to do it, at least not yet. It'd peer through the door almost always accompanied by the malformed monstrosity that resembles my little girl. It makes me sick.

That horrid creature's neck, when it did peer in on my work, would crack with grotesque colorization as the doorway would crack along with it, and with every visitation, it would torment me with what tormented me the most, the visualization of sound that'd flash in my head when the being would weep from the doorway. Its neck crippled under its own length—explaining the cracks' violent rhythm.

The tears crashed on the wooden floorboards like melancholy clouds of a coming storm. You knew it was coming, but it often lingered in the distance just in earshot. Her eyes bloodshot as if resembling sorrow that also tore at its being. My heart was often broken at the sight—if not terrified.

Disgust.

Why was I subjugated with the thought of sadness as I stared at her face? Her dried-out, hay-like hair often stuck to the dried-up splotches of tears on her face. Her hair would mesh with the darkness behind her. Her skin—gray and shriveled—swallowed her eyes, leaving black pools. I'd imagine her skin would feel like a decayed foreskin, and yet I feel I'm tied to her as much as she is to me, cursed for a damned eternity.

What popped out from the darkness underneath her was a revolting lump of flesh that looked to carry pus-filled blemishes on its skin like that of a dragon with its scales, but its eyes untethered by the gross afflictions that riddled its existence looked so sad and innocent as it clenched onto an item so tight, it was too damaged to tell what it was—the item. It looked to have seen centuries of bacteria as layers upon layers of black mold crusted on it. I'd say the smell was nauseating, but I believe my sense of smell died a long time ago.

These eyes—so big—on this tiny monstrosity also twinkled with tears making me feel sorry for the visage behind me. They looked to be conjoined at the hip as each time they often arrived together. They just lingered behind the weathered door.

Click, Clack

My fingers only type harder, and harder, the noise of my own endeavors wash away the horrid atmosphere—I hope, at least. The distraction is all I live for, but then the creak of the door would ricochet again in my general direction. Then I'd snap - a tormented rage with tears as I'd slap my hands on the desk—time and time again. I'd often repeat the process of this prison-like nightmare, and I'd utter the same words—or something of equal disgust, "Leave me, you horrid abominations. Leave me to my Hell. Just go, you disgusting, revolting obstrocities! If I'm trapped here, then I'd prefer to be trapped in solitude! Loneliness will be my tomb..." Then my tone would soften, and with tears, I'd weep, "Then at least I wouldn't suffer the constant remembrance."

My tears would echo like impatient fingers on wood. My desk wore from the many other tears shed. Then that's when those melancholy creatures would close the door again to later check on me again, and again and again—it's been an eternity... Or at least, it felt as such. Then I'd break into a fret wail as I'd crash my head into my arms. My sorrow is my own...

• • •

A mother waited with her child in the other room as the doctor, who was called to the house, made his usual rounds. He came back with a grim look on his face. "What is it, Doctor?" The mother longed for good news, but alas, she wasn't expecting such.

The doctor sighed as he flipped through his paperwork on the patient. "It's not looking good, Anneliese. The machines at this point are just sustaining his vegetable state; there is little brain activity. It's been years, and your funds are dwindling..." He took a deep breath before continuing, "Anneliese, it's time. You need to pull the plug. I'm concerned. At this rate, you're going to be left broke and homeless. Think of your daughter."

The truth rang in her ear like a deafening shock of electricity. Fear and sorrow overwhelmed her, and she burst out crying. Her daughter clenched onto her babydoll in a concerned manner, nearly on the brink of tears as well.

"So Daddy isn't getting better, Mommy?" She tugged at her mother's dress.

"No, dear, but don't worry. He'll be off to a better place soon," she reassured her daughter, trying to hide her sorrow through a forced smile as tears rained down her cheeks like a silent storm.

This broke the dam, and the child's eyes overflowed with tears of buried sadness. She kept strong for Mommy for a while, but it was about time for hope to shatter. The doctor navigated the mother to the other room, as the daughter accompanied them. They needed closure, and this was about to cut the thread that held this family back in pain for years now, nearly half a decade. The tears shed won't be the last.

• • •

The monsters that linger outside the door whispered words like incantations I can't fathom. I couldn't make out the muffled demonic words uttered by these creatures, and I'm not sure I care to know. The voices echoed around me like a curse. I would say I'm used to this Hell, but it felt different like a change was conspiring.

I stopped my typing—the chatter was approaching. I stood up, but my back was left facing the doorway. Something arose in me, something different like a sense of peace. I couldn't explain it, but it was time.

Creeeaakk

What arose gave way to understanding. I planned to turn around, and I did. The usual sounds of my horror weren't there. The creatures weren't there. Finally, a visage of beauty I had long forgotten stood before me. My family mere feet away swallowed the strong stench of melancholy, and it was replaced with longing relief. Tears swelled up in my eyes just as it did in theirs. My wife's black locks—like the creature—stuck to her cheek in dried up splotches of grief, and the child no longer held the black mold infested object, but rather, she held a doll close to her heart. The last gift I gave before the accident… I remember now.

Their eyes look beautiful as they gleam through the flood. I wanted to run to them in a sprint, and hug them immensely, but I felt fixated on this spot. I couldn't move, but I am content. I knew what was transpiring… Closure. They approach ever so softly—step-by-step. I now laid on a bed, staring up at the ceiling. They now stood before me, and I awaited the words. The ones I'd hope to hear.

"Hey, love," she choked up, and the daughter continued to stay silent due to what I believe was nervousness and sorrow accompanied by uneasy tension. Her heart raced along her mother's. "I know I only came in here to check up on you. It was just too hard to gaze on your predicament. I still just feel so ashamed. This was all my fault…" She broke into a sob. "I was supposed to pick her up—maybe—just maybe, if I had that truck wouldn't have hit you."

By this point, my wife was basically yelling at herself indirectly. Telling herself lies to cope with the truth because she needed someone to blame. Her tear ducts started to run dry, and she started to grasp onto some clarity. "But after all these years, I realized nothing could be done. I love you, honey, but I know it's probably not fair to you—or to us—so it's time we all let you rest."

I, from beyond their plain, shed the last of my lingering emotions with a single tear. My hatred began to flee into forgiveness and love. They began to reach for the plug as the doctor laid his hand on my wife's shoulder to ease her hesitation. Then with a burst my daughter lunged onto my remaining existence, and started to bawl her eyes out. Getting to see this last moment freed me from the weight of my passing.

My wife gave my daughter a second before losing herself again to the sobbing. The doctor was accepting, and didn't push the issue. I could see he was truly helping my family. "Okay, dear, it's time to say goodbye to Daddy." She stepped back off of me, and hid her tears from everyones' gaze with the dolly I gave her.

The doctor continued to console my wife by comforting her in her effort to pull the plug. It'd be better for all of us. The plane in which I was suspended was like in a state of limbo; limbo is like having a foot in the grave, and the other in a ghost-like reality. My existence, I could feel it fading. Even though I laid in bed, I felt as if I were standing before her as she leaned in for a kiss on my forehead. I could feel her tears crash upon my lifeless corpse—or at least it might as well be so.

Her hand reached for the plug as she pulled her lips away leaving the last beautiful impression of her for me. She whispered into my ear with the last words I'd ever experience. "I'll always love you." Then the plug was pulled.

A fabrication of a tear rolled down my face of my lingering essence as if I felt a sense of calming. My body fluttered like butterflies dispersing from a field as I donned a smile, but it all became torment. My eyes widened at the last seconds of ceaselessness. As my last fragments of existence evaporated into the great beyond, I saw a regretful sight. Why had I been so blind?! What currently reflected off the gleam of eyes that gave way to my realization is this. My last true sight beheld the doctor muttering what looked to be di-rected right at me.

I read his lips, and they reverberated a soundless echo of horror. "Now at long last—she is mine."

The Childhood Fears of Chris Crow

The Decrepit Staircase

Nightmares—dreams encased in terror. Sometimes you suffer the torment until you feel the death of yourself in the dream. When I was a fledgling, I had many of these. I was tormented by relatives and friends alike to watch horror movies that terrified me. I'd wander in the night with cold sweats hoping that the visages that manifested in the dark weren't real. This is an early fear I often revisited as a fledgling, and now I pass it on to you.

• • •

The house I stood before in a hazy existence—in a state of limbo—was probably replicated by other houses that dwell in my memory. I often recall a mangy, red brick house. It often resembled that of my grandparents; old house before the move at the age of five. I don't recall the faces of those involved—I only remember blurs. The interior was also very vague.

The only thing that stood out was that damnable staircase that lingered in my youthful mind all those years ago. I remember it clear as day. The doorway to it lingered in the back of this nightmare. Everything seemed natural and normal until I walked through this neglected doorway. It leads to a sight that would make anyone burst with unexpected tension and fear. What laid beyond this entrance to anxiety-induced fear was a massively dark pit that was outlined by a square-like descension of a staircase.

The staircase was a makeshift cluster of different woods—covered in splinters—as it descended into oblivion. I'd recall my heart palpitating intensely in my chest as I took each step at a time. My heart weighed heavy as my head became lightheaded. My feet weren't any better. They felt light, almost like glass, that if I weren't pushing forward through the eerie hellscape, that I might shatter, and plummet to my doom.

I'd hear the creaks and cracks of the wood as I'd descend into darkness. Why a little one of my youth at the time would covet an idea is beyond comprehension. The heart pained with anxiety and fear of the unknown as each step was taken lightly. Like an optical illusion, the stairs may have seemed like forever, but I reached the bottom with ease.

The descent was the easy part, but the true terror that lingered on my psyche like a festering wound was what laid at the bottom. A decrepit hall awaited me with cobwebs and dust-fueled darkness. How I managed to see was beyond me, but in a dream anything is possible— even in a nightmare. The wood looked to be on the verge of collapse, and the walls felt like they'd enclose you as you continued to progress through the claustrophobia-induced paranoia. The wood resembled charcoal as if its appearance inherited the gloom of this eerie aura.

But what was to unfold at the end of this tour from Hell was the sarcophagus glinted in gold linings and design. The head of a pharaoh rested in the design of this object as it stood up leaned against the dead-end of the hall. I was small, and I'd stare up at this face. It looked to stare back. Mesmerized by why I've been guided to this desolate abyss, I stood—paralyzed. By this point, the fear was crippling. I had no control over my motor skills. I couldn't even twitch as my eyes just laid wide open. Sweat coated my soft, young exterior as the sarcophagus slowly creaked open. My heart skipped a beat.

I felt dead. Chills shivered across me like if I were exposed to a blizzard— so suddenly. I breathed heavily as tears collected in my eyes like a dam on the verge of combustion. The flood was imminent as the contents of the sarcophagus became visible. As tales of Egyptian mummification rapidly came to mind, I saw the aged and tattered rags of a corpse step out from the blackened abyss that was once merely an ancient coffin. Its eyes filled with crimson peered into my soul. I could smell the rot. I was petrified by most of my senses: my nose burned with disgust to the point I wanted to gag, my eyes dried up from the lack of blinking in fear of losing sight of the horror, and my body fatigued due to the dumping of glutamate.

I shook in a sense where I was still frozen to a spot, but my body still vibrated like a car engine; however, I wasn't going anywhere. It staggered with each step, limbs cracking due to decay. It shuffled its feet which combined with the sickening sound effects caused a very fearful and unnerving terror to chill my very veins. I was so miniscule, and all of this caused my youthful essence to be thwarted by the slow closing in of the creature's distance between us.

It moaned violently as it stretched its arms towards me. Closer... And closer... And closer until the trapped air from its body was even able to be felt upon my face. Then... I awoke. I'd lay awake gasping at the sheets, to the air I breathed, and my eyes would dilate from the unexpected fear. At such a young age, it all felt so real.

I would dream of this nightmare for many moons, but it would return after some time has passed. After I aged, it got to the point that I manifested this nightmare into another dream that would occur. I'd fall in love with a family that manifested in that house, and the door would soon be sealed. After several times I lived through this dream, it'd get to the point it was unrecognizable, but to this day, I miss what that dream gave me. It wasn't merely a childhood fear, but rather a lesson to be learned.

Evelyn

It felt dark and lonely in a house of three. Evelyn was a young girl that lived alone with her middle-aged parents. But she had no siblings, and no friends. The loneliness left her mind racing with possibilities and fantasies, so she imagined herself a perfect little friend, Amber. She seemed so real to young Evelyn, and her parents paid no mind because they were too busy creating a cure for their daughter in the basement, leaving no time for the family to bond. She wasn't able to go outside because of the fear of death that lurked out there in the expansive world she was never a part of.

Amber looked nearly identical to herself because Evelyn saw no one more as a friend than herself, being that she rarely sees her parents as is or anyone else for that matter. Amber appeared one afternoon out of nowhere on an average day filled with tears. Evelyn was crying immensely merely at the thought of the piercing loneliness that darkened her mind. Maybe that was the reason she snapped, and Amber was born. Children usually grow out of having imaginary friends by three or four, but Amber manifested at around six years old.

"Don't cry. I know it can be hard, but you need to be positive about all this. That it all has a reason, and one day you'll have as many friends as you want. But for now, Evelyn, I'll be your friend. We can be like sisters." The fascination giggled with a smile that lit the trauma that weighed heavily on Evelyn.

Strange thought that she didn't fear this stranger before her. She just smiled back, and felt an unusual comfort emanating from her. The waterworks stopped, and she said back to her, "I know I should be frightened that you resemble me and know my name, but I know I'm probably just losing my mind. But my mom and dad will fix my illness soon. They're scientists—doctors—and they'll cure me, and I'll not need to feel so alone anymore."

"Well, until then, you have me, and I'll be your bestest friend in the world, almost like a sister. My name's Amber." She held a huge but friendly smile upon her face as she held her hand out towards Evelyn. She grasped Amber's hand limply, not expecting to feel it, but it actually felt all too real. It was almost as if she had muscle memory, as if she'd held this hand before, but that wasn't possible. Her mind must have made the fabricated vision all too real, meaning her psyche must have had its last straw, and snapped her into realism. Amber was real—or at least to her.

The next morning after Amber manifested, Evelyn awoke to her watching her sleep. She just sat Indian-style in front of the bed with her face resting in her hands, and her elbows resting in her lap. "Good morning, has anyone ever told you how beautiful you are when you sleep? I've never experienced sleep, but if it were an Olympic sport you'd take the gold," Amber flattered her as she laid groggy in bed.

The flattery was welcomed by Evelyn because her parents weren't very attentive of her, being that saving her by staying locked away in a basement nearly 24/7 was the only way they could express their love for her, nearly isolating her alone. "Thank you. It's kinda nice finally having someone there for you. I love my parents, don't get me wrong, but I also hate them." She sat up in bed, and stared forward with a melancholy look upon her face and continued, "I've never seen the outside. The windows are sealed and covered. And I've never felt the warm sensation of the sun or even seen the outside color of my house. I've only ever read the health and science books that riddle this house and/or play with my dolls that my mother buys for me on occasion, but of course, those presents are also occupied by some Lysol wipes and rubber gloves because my parents are too afraid they'll contaminate me. No physical contact unless we are in the lab, but half the time it's the damn needles, not a hug or a kiss." She started to tear up and huddled into a fetal position.

Amber popped up right beside her in an instant. She wrapped her arms around Evelyn in an attempt to ease her pain with what she desperately needed, physical contact. She felt warm, almost like real body warmth, and her touch was almost too comforting as if she were her real parents, her closest friend, and protector. "I'll never leave you, Evelyn, I'll always be here. You don't need to cry anymore. You have all you ever wanted now, and I'll give you everything you need. I'm here for you." Amber squeezed harder and buried her head into Evelyn's shoulder, and then mumbled again. "I will never leave you. Never." Amber's breath felt scorching hot on her shoulder as she spoke through Evelyn's shirt.

"Honey, breakfast is ready!" Her mom called out from around the corridor, and from the kitchen.

A little smile peeked out from her face as Amber loosened her grip on her. "I know this 'breakfast'," Evelyn air quoted breakfast, "is just an opportunity for them to give me perhaps another present to butter me up because they are about to stick needles in me again." She looked sad again.

"Go, this may be your only moment with your parents. I never had parents, yet it feels all too familiar having some. So I'll wait here. It's time for them to shine now." Amber's words were so soothing, bringing another smile to Evelyn's face. She jumped out of her bed, threw on her PJs, and then made her way to the kitchen.

"Your eggs are getting—" said her mom before getting cut-off by her in mid-sentence.

"I'm here, Mom," she said as she quickly sat down.

"You seem energetic. I'm happy to hear it, and Mom's got a surprise after this for you!" her mom said with a smile as she sat down at the kitchen table across from Evelyn.

She sat her plate on the table as Evelyn began again, but in a rather unappreciative tone, "Yeah, I know, Mother, more tests and more shots."

"Don't be like that, sweetie. You know your father and I are looking to cure you of this terrible disease. One day you'll be able—" Her mother tried to calm her before being interrupted by her.

"Yea! Able to do what?! Actually go outside, or make friends? And where is Dad anyways? Probably in that fucking lab again!" Evelyn crossed her arms in a pout.

"Evelyn! Your father has worked tirelessly for years. We're so close, dear. Just please…" Her mom almost broke into tears.

"I'm sorry, Mom. Don't cry." She felt guilty.

She wiped her tears and smiled at her daughter. "I know, sweetheart. Now let me get you that present, and we can head down to the lab after you finish your meal. Dig in." They both ate, giving each other glances once in a while when they looked up from their plates. Her mom gave smiles to ensure a pleasant experience before the inevitable pain to follow. "You know you can make small talk with Mommy. You don't have to just eat. We have time before." Her mom tried to spark a conversation.

"No, Mom, I'm done. We best just get this over with." Evelyn looked sorrowful as if she weren't looking forward to the seemingly endless trials before her. Every day to every week, there were only the same events, tests, and false affection. But she longed for the day her parents would cure her, and then they could all enjoy the world outside together.

Her mother was still not pleased with Evelyn's tone, only felt saddened because she knew she was only hurting her daughter more every day. "Evelyn, dear, put on your gloves before opening your present. We may have decontaminated it, but you can't be too careful. Oh, and don't forget your mask, too, before we head down to the lab," her mother said while leading her to the front room with a present in hand. She sat down on the plastic-wrapped couch in the living room after putting on the gloves that laid beside her on the end table. Her mother brought her the present from the kitchen and she handed it to her, placing it on Evelyn's lap.

"Ow, I wonder what it is?" Evelyn spoke sarcastically, because at this point she generally didn't care.

Her mom seemed too excited, but Evelyn grew distracted—and who stood blankly in the back was Amber. While her mother jumped with an unusual enthusiasm, it felt as if time stood still. Then Amber was gone when their eyes locked with a stare.

"Awe, come on, dear, don't leave me in suspense." Her mother broke her out of a trance. Evelyn often felt a slight ominous nature behind Amber, but she came off as quite gentle.

"Okay, Mom," she said while distracted like she was previously in a daze. She began to shuffle into the gift bag she was given to reveal the mystery. The present put her at unease because it was a twin set of dolls, one with dark hair and the other with blonde. She knew her mother was unaware of Amber, but it still was chilling.

"Do you like it, dear?" Her mom said, hoping for some love or praise from her daughter.

"Yeah, I do," Evelyn answered back with a fake but convincing smile.

"Great, I knew you would. Now hurry along. Your father is waiting." She gestured to her daughter toward the kitchen where the basement door led to the lab.

On their way to the kitchen, she noticed an eye that peeked from the darkness of her room. It loomed intensely on her, and she knew she had to quench Amber with her attention. She realized she had forgotten her mask, a great excuse to break away to console Amber's intensity. "Mom, I forgot my mask!" She made it seem so important with a sense of shock.

"You're right, honey! I'll wait in the kitchen. Just hurry along, your father shouldn't be kept waiting," her mother agreed, seeing it as very important that she has it.

Evelyn rushed toward her room down the hall to keep Amber a secret. Her mask laid on the end table past her cradle which she used for her dolls. She had to turn on the light to see when she entered the room. Then in a shocking, dreadful moment as the lights flickered on, the spectre stood directly in front of her, causing her to fling back into the door making a crashing sound echo throughout the house.

"You okay, honey?" Her mom was concerned by the sudden massive thump.

"Yeah, I'm fine. I just accidentally slammed the door pretty hard," she yelled down the hall really quickly. She turned back around, and Amber still stood there with a cutesy smile.

"Wanna play? I noticed you haven't been paying attention to me, and I'm bored." She jumped in excitement. "Oh, what's that? Are those new toys?!" It was basically a rhetorical question. Amber then snatched the dolls from Evelyn, and opened the packaging the rest of the way.

"Hey! I'm not here to play. You need to be more careful. What if my mom would have seen you?" she grilled her sporadically, taking breaths in between each sentence.

"It's not like I'd let her, but if I had, I would have to devour her." At first Amber seemed serious as she paused with a stern stare, then broke out in laughter. "Just kidding."

Evelyn held a nervous smile on her face, almost chuckling due to uneasiness. Her heart dropped in her chest, and dread crept in instantly, like if her heart was set into a pool of fear. She felt like she was drowning in eerie tension. She feared for what Amber was, but also for what she felt. She still cared for this suspicious entity that manifested itself, clinging to her because she was her only friend, but Amber didn't fill her with confidence.

"So can we play?" Amber broke the silence with a smile.

"We can when I get back, but for now, you can play with my new dolls until I return," Evelyn offered because she needed to keep her docile.

"Fine, I'll wait," Amber gave her a pouty face, "but I don't need both." She tossed the blonde doll to the floor, and stared intensely at the dark-haired one. "I really like this one."

Evelyn then left the room with caution after easing herself past her to grab her mask. Amber never took her eyes off the doll as she played with it. Evelyn then made her way to the kitchen.

She managed to put her mask on right as she entered the kitchen. "What took you so long, dear?" Her mother looked perplexed. "Did you lose it? I told you to keep it where you can find it."

"Yeah, I guess I did," she lied while averting her eyes from her mother's.

"I told you we shouldn't keep your father waiting. Let's get a move on, hun," she practically, and in a gentle manner, pushed her daughter down the basement stairs.

The descending of the staircase was filled with creaks, and blackness besides the light that protruded from behind a barely opened, metal vault-like door at the bottom of the sairs. This feeling that sounded inside Evelyn's heart beat like a percussion instrument as she gripped her chest. Her fear of the dark only existed when she had to navigate down these janky floorboards below her feet. What lurked within these few steps? Her mind wandered away from her with thoughts of what frightening things could be.

A crooked smile showed through her mind's eye with a creepy cackle like that of a sinister laughter with a hint of pleasure, or joy. She imagined a colorful figure skulking from beneath the stairs. The frightening visage resembled that of a carnival clown, but its arms slinked like snakes twisting about the floorboards. Her anxiety quickly turned to dread as she imagined the hands of this clown nearing her feet.

Then a small spider dangled in front of Evelyn as she snapped out of her nightmarish imagination. It only built on the fear she manifested. She quickly lunged back to avoid the horrid arachnid that crawled from its web only an inch from her face. It caused her to lose her footing, and she began to fall.

Her mom was closely behind, and leapt to her aid to grab her arm quickly enough to where Evelyn was pulled back into her mother's arms just in time. As her mother—with fear in both their eyes—coddled her because of her near plummet, "Dear," she gasped for breath at the initial event, "you need to be more careful." Her mother clasped her head as she suffered the adrenaline that coursed through her veins, petting her head to comfort her daughter. This ordeal revealed further the extent of Evelyn's mom's love, but this only strengthened the apathy she harbored toward her mother. Only if she were around more than this, around longer than a few needle shots.

Then that's when the apathetic Evenlyn was caressed with an eerie presence like goosebumps on the soul. She peered over her mother's shoulder, as her mother flattened her hair with every stroke, to widen her eyes in uneasiness. Amber stood at the top of the stairs with an amusing smirk plastered on her face, but all she did was speak with a giggle and mutter, "Have a nice fall?"

She was sarcastic with a malicious undertone as if she were toying with her, like if she gathered amusement from her fright, yet Evelyn could still feel a warm, gentle essence from Amber as if a sense of familiarity kept them connected. And with a blink, Amber vanished as quickly as she appeared, and then at that instant, Evelyn's mother broke the tension. "Come on, sweetie, your father is waiting."

Evelyn was shaken to the point that her anxiety swallowed her voice. She merely nodded as her mother faintly smiled, and led her to the lab by taking her hand. Evelyn was starting to bite on her nails from under her mask as she entered the claustrophobic laboratory that was cluttered with beakers, vials, chemicals, and research galore. Papers were scattered across the desk, making it hard to perceive that there was a computer under the mess. A screensaver of pipes whirled and twined on the screen letting all know the age of the computer, but their common source of activity, that most of their research laid, was on the laptop, probably locked away from prying eyes.

But there lingered an ominous sheet that separated the rest of the lab from what was accessible to Evelyn. Her parents didn't even allow her to step near the plastic that draped away the last undiscovered bastion of this isolated prison she lived in. Since she was young, that section was withheld from her, mocking her, and why her parents defended it so only bore a curious cat out of her.

But her attention then snapped back to her father's presence that peered at her level initiating a conversation. "Hello, my darling girl, you ready for another checkup? I know you're not too keen on this, but I know my brave little girl," then he couldn't help but end on a baby voice, almost mocking—in a sense—as he finished with a 'my little girl is too adorable' face, "isn't afraid of needles. "

He patronized her. She didn't see herself as such. She saw herself as an adult, but she'd always be daddy's little girl. She was still shaken from Amber, so she only nodded her head as she prepared for her daily injection.

The cold embrace of the alcohol wipe caressing her arm began the anxiety she now felt. Her heart started to speed up with every second the needle drew nearer to her fragile skin as the idea burrowed into her mind; it never got easier. "You're just going to feel a pinch, but you already know that," her father inspected the needle in full preparation for the injection.

It felt as if it were getting hotter with every pressing second that she was spared the experience of this next experiment. Every session was merely a test run as every day was an inevitable prick of blood shed for another failure to be cataloged, but the parents never gave up because it drove them—Evelyn feeling an ominous intent. The needle inched ever closer, but her gaze now turned to the nuisance that she called her friend.

The gleam of the fluorescent light that hung high above the lab shone brightly on the needle tip as Evelyn's anxiety was redirected. Amber beckoned a look with her tugging on the sheet like a dog longing to enter the house after being left in the rain—a desperate whine that shone so hastily in her stare. Amber wasn't even fixated on Evelyn, and the procedure. But the eerie desire made Evelyn feel uneasy.

"Ow!" She didn't see the needle penetrate her skin. Her focus lay on the increasing intensity that drew her attention because now the curiosity no longer laid dormant. She, too, wanted to know what was covered in secrecy. The sheet took on a spectre-like presence as it slightly rippled due to the air conditioner that lay overhead. The action of such tantalizion of her peripherals, the eyes would dart back and forth from parent to sheet as the injection would finish up.

"All done, sweetie," her father spoke gently as he placed a Band-Aid on her wound. He stood up with a smile as he removed his latex gloves. "Okay, now your mom will escort you up the stairs while I finish up down here. You were once again so brave. I'm so proud of you." He smiled, and then turned to tend to his research.

"Okay, Evelyn, dear, time to go upstairs, and play." Her mother started to nudge her out along with her, but Evelyn's sight was only drawn to what she just recently obsessed over, the sheet. And Amber only seemed to stand there lifeless, but her obsession only became an extension of Evelyn's, for she grew to further imitate Amber's expression more eminently inside.

Evelyn puzzled over what could lay behind the sheet, but what also became more concerning was Amber's creepy antics. They were ominous, but her intentions were shown true when the piercing sensation darkened Evelyn's heart. Were these emotions what Amber felt? It was fear, curiosity, and—most of all—an emptying feeling of dread almost like Amber knew what lay within reach. Evelyn could feel the tug at her chest as she gripped it. It was consuming her. Were these her fears, or was this why Amber started to warp?

"What are you thinking about?" Evelyn shot up with a fright. She was merely contemplating to herself as she sat with her back against the couch. Amber now seemed more collective then she had previously acted.

"Nothing," Evelyn lied back.

Amber just smirked. She knew something... Or felt something... "Alright, keep your secrets, but you know you can't hide anything from your best friend," she finished with a genuinely happy smile.

Evelyn began to calm her rapid heartbeat. It didn't last long. It peaked at the fright, and decreased by the time of the smile, almost like Amber could manipulate her feelings.

"So what do you wanna play?" Amber spoke again, but seemingly, completely she had forgotten their interactions in the last hour. Why would her emotions flip so evidently if her prior ambitions were to uncover the secret of the lab sheet? Or maybe, it was herself.

Evelyn started to realize that Amber was only an extension. If she wanted to know the secret, Amber would want it, too—or at least that is what she had hypothesized. "What about an expedition?" she had suggested to her. "Like... uhm." She wet her lips in anxiousness like if the idea were exhilarating, but yet fearful.

"Like an adventure?!" Amber hopped up in excitement with a gleam in her gaze.

"Yeah, something like that." She smiled, hiding her facetious nature disregarding the serious issue that would unfold. She decided to turn the discovery into a game, but such an action would discredit her kind posterior because she was about to break the only rules her parents had given her.

Amber couldn't hold it. Her excitement bursted into a yelp-like squeal as she shook her hands which were balled up to hold back some of the outburst. "What are we doing?! Where are we going?"

The longing to know was always lingering within her, and it only swelled until a child's curiosity compelled her. Evelyn beckoned Amber with a gesture of her hand as she snuck into the kitchen compelling Amber to tail her.

"Oow, this is exciting," Amber rejoiced as she just played along.

"Okay." Now Evelyn thought of something outrageous of the current speculations about Amber's existence. Could she work as a distraction? Was she real enough to cause a crash of dishes to topple, distracting Evelyn's mother? This was the start of Evelyn's rebellious revelation as this was the climax to her life. "I'm going to need you, Amber, to cause the dishes to fall, but not until I'm within eyeshot of my mother, so I won't be suspected. But also, I can't make a move until my father leaves the lab."

She started to trail off, almost as if talking to herself, but it was clear Amber listened. Her glee contorted to a wicked smirk as if the mischievous nature of this heist illuminated her heart with joy like a house on fire. Just the thought of conspiring to express enlightenment, caressed with anxiety and terror of what to come, was evident on Amber's face as the singular thought of the AC rippling the sheet in the lab tainted Evelyn with every second the heist commenced.

"I'll do my best. This is going to be fun," Amber muttered to herself as her face now resembled the tense face Evelyn held. This was the moment. Her mother now stood in the kitchen, but only steps from the door. She needed to get the door open first, so the crash could distract the father as well.

Amber was in position, she held up a thumbs up. "Mom!" A simple yelp was all that was needed to coerce her mother's attention.

"Yes, dear, what's wrong?" she said to her daughter's cry. With the patting of Evelyn's hair, her mother always seemed to care when she wasn't busy; perhaps it could be the guilt that tore at her for the lack of attention she gave.

"I just don't feel good, Mommy," she said convincingly, mimicking someone sick.

"Was it the shot, sweetie?" She was concerned because she doesn't often show symptoms after a test, but to make her mother believe it may just be a tummy ache, she shook her head and rubbed her stomach—cutely.

"No, I think it was something I ate. I feel bloated," and as Evelyn finished, Amber struggled to manifest herself into a physical state. She desperately tried with such ambition. Strain showed across her face as it took immense determination for a specter—of sorts—to merely touch something not of her plane.

"Okay, I'll get you some gas prevention medication from the bathroom, dear," her mother said concernedly, still considering the injection is reacting to her. Then, as the mother nearly left her daughter's field of vision, a crash penetrated the ears of those near. "What the—?"

That got her attention, but the door wasn't ajar, so Evelyn would have to use some other means to pry her father from his research. Since she was steps away from her mother, her mother only glanced at her before losing herself to puzzlement as she made her way to the mess. "What on Earth? I thought I had stacked you well." She stood over the mess while scratching her head in bewilderment.

Evelyn's opportunity was golden, and she had slipped through the basement door during the confusion. Her mother though still held on to a sliver of consciousness of the situation, and glanced back for a moment. She didn't see Evelyn right away, but assumed she ran off to acquire the meds she spoke of. So she cleaned up the dishes that dressed the floor in hazards.

This was Evelyn's first time down the rickety stairs alone. She was often accompanied by a parent, but only when another test was necessary. The thought would cause her to feel a phantom sting in her forearm as a form of repressed trauma, even something so small as it accumulates could cause detriment on a minor scale. With each step, a creak would sound off, and visions of terrors her little mind could fathom made themselves known. Her anxiety skyrocketed, but she held true. Her bravery masked her internal struggle as she reached the last step.

Hopefully her mother was still cleaning, she thought, as she started to peer into the lab. Her father was gripping his head as he seemingly flustered over the diagram upon his laptop screen. It looked to be chemical compounds broken down as they react to an external reactant—her blood... To no avail, it seems he had failed again to cure his daughter's affliction.

In this moment, as cheeky as it may be, Evelyn concocted a devious plan, but the continued lies started to weigh on her—but not as much as her spiteful curiosity consumed. The fear was overwhelming, but also exciting. "Dad! Mommy's hurt!" She was positive this deceit would prevail.

"What?!" He shot up dramatically. He came to her side, gripping both of her shoulders before asking, "What happened?!" He came off as frantic.

But she only retorted with, "Well, she was bleeding, Daddy," which resulted in him acknowledging her remark hastily as he seemingly flew up the stairs.

"Don't touch anything, honey. I'll be right back," he urged quickly before departing.

She only nodded. She didn't have but a second to answer in return, so with his departure, she sealed the door with haste, and concluded with her scheme. She'd only have a slight moment of peace before her parents would tear down the door in disappointment, and frustration with increasing anger with every minute that'd pass by.

As she stepped closer to the veil of no return—the sheet that separated her from the unknown. Amber joined in the splendor a mere minute after her father raced frantically upstairs.

"Do it! You know you want to. You've always wanted to," Amber spoke with a pleasurable expression as she was pleased by the plan's accomplishment, but yet even though she actually held an expression of anxiousness, Evelyn, too, was pleased with herself.

"I thought you'd want to do the honors." She tried to quell her curiosity, but it seemed she had something else in mind.

"No, I got you this far, but it's you who must make this journey," Amber finished.

Evelyn now saw, in all its glory, Amber's purpose. She was created for this moment. This was a swelling on her psyche, and all her emotions compiling into a fascination—or was it? But with every second, she only questioned more.

"I'm scared." Evelyn's heart raced, and as she paced ever so closely to pulling back the veil, the gripping on her heart tightened leaving a dry sensation in her mouth as she bit her lips anxiously.

Dread—knowing why she was here, but not knowing may be better. The terror of not knowing though won in the end as for not knowing in general led her on this path. "No need to be afraid, I'm right here with you." Amber laid her hand on her shoulder to coax her into pulling the sheet to reveal what they longed to see.

Her hand was cold. Dread continued to creep on her as the sensation sent shivers down her spine. It was like she was dead. It was even more eerie when it was accompanied by the caressing of her guiding hand. Evelyn never felt her touch before, besides the realization of when Amber was first concepted...

The thought was interrupted by a loud bang. A repetition of thuds echoed from the door. Her parents laid beyond the threshold. "Honey, open the door!" Her mother spoke first with a desperately frantic tone with hints of genuine concern. "Your father and I aren't mad. Just please open the door!"

"This is not funny, Evelyn Marie Mavericks. Open this door right now!" Her father uttered with a rage consumed with concern because Evelyn's parents were worried about her behavior of late, and the fact that she stood alone in a place littered with hazardous materials.

"Don't turn back now. We were having so much fun." Amber's tone was soft, almost sinister, as she whispered ominously into her ear. "Now let's pull back this curtain, and resume the show!" Amber's fingers clenched into the sheet as she ripped it from its suspension. She was seemingly growing more powerful. At this point, it was becoming more difficult to resist the hold Amber held on Evelyn almost as if Amber's mind were slowly seeping into control.

The uneasy tension of the anxious nature of the situation started to tear away at Evelyn. She panted rapidly as she tried to steady her breathing, but the sudden unveiling of the hidden section put a shock to her system. Her legs began to buckle as she fell prey to the manipulation that curiosity invoked. At this point, it felt as if her free will were stricken from her as she stumbled toward Amber's siren song.

But her siren song was one of silence. Amber now stood directly in front of a capsule of sorts that was illuminated by a faint glow of emerald. Evelyn inched ever closer, but her nerves flared up like violent goosebumps. Something didn't feel right... If a feeling could hurt with mere mention, it was this one. Internally she screamed, "Run," with every fiber of her fight-or-flight, but she was no longer in control. Fate—or perhaps destiny—overrode her survival instinct, if she ever had it.

Amber began to sob, but with every step from Evelyn, Amber accompanied that cry with a faint laughter. Shear dread struck her heart as she couldn't fight the pull Amber had on her—or perhaps—was it a tug on her heart? The sorrow that Eevelyn would seemingly expel on her face drowned her cheeks as she had yet to experience the horror Amber dwelled on... Then it stopped...

The weeping was no more, but the laughter weakened Evelyn's hold on her balance. Her legs nearly collapsed at the overwhelming adrenaline that seeped into her by the terrifying spectacle.

...Then that, too, stopped.

"Have you ever wondered what it's like to be dead?" Amber spoke, and broke the moment of eerie silence.

Evelyn gulped as her voice felt strangled by the fear of uttering a sound. A meek voice came from her mouth. "Uhm, what are you saying?" She could barely speak as her voice was assaulted by the sorrowful choking that nearly overcame her bravery.

"It was you… Always you, their love was always yours." She stood inhumanly as she didn't move a single inch even when talking. She would repeat that over and over again like a sickening chant, gradually getting louder with every mutter.

"Amber?" She tried to comfort, but was ultimately too shaken by the ominous display. She always knew that she was supernatural in essence, but this moment felt malicious.

"WHY WAS IT ALWAYS YOU!!!" Amber's tone was now demonic in nature, and Evelyn only stood paralyzed, especially now that she could see the horror that set Amber off.

A fetus hovered in a jar connected to a monitor that read the contents as it coded formulas theorized to cure Evelyn's affliction, a system designed by her parents—with a panel that read, 'Amber Lillian Mavericks.' Amber's real form was displayed grotesquely as her skin didn't carry much left of human characteristics. Her skin—all over—was penetrated and warped from the vegetation that grew within, and around her form revealing a parasitic codependency.

The plant kept her alive… And impeded her growth, forever and ever suspended in a state of infancy.

"I had to live through you. It wasn't all bad. In a way, we are one of the same. We're twins, and you probably wondered why I manifested in your mind…" She took a moment to smile as she tried not to give away the surprise too suddenly. "Because, my lovely sis, I'm what kept you alive. I've been growing inside you like a vaccine… But with enough of me, we could be whole."

At this point, Evelyn was devastated, torn emotionally and mentally—breaking down with every revelation. "No wonder," Evelyn muttered to herself with whatever air could escape her lungs to produce a rebuttal, but she didn't know where she began and Amber's mind ended. She actually agreed, and began to accept.

"And with this," Amber's form was now strong enough to take control, and she then picked up a syringe that did lay mere inches from her incubator, "with more of me injected into you, we can live together in peace."

Her words were tainted because with any consciousness left of Evelyn's hold told her with a sharp anxiousness that lingered, like a spark of light forever trapped in a dark void, was that Amber's words were malicious with revenge-filled intent. And she was just buying time in Evelyn's subconscious until the time she could manifest in real form. Will Evelyn fade when Amber corrodes her soul, or would Evelyn just become just like her?

…Or will she just cease to exist?…

Then Evelyn's hand moved on its own like a marionette nudged by its strings. She seemingly—compulsively—moved of her own accord, both consciousnesses interlocked into one single impulse. As Amber implicated her desires onto Evelyn's, increasing with every motion, Evelyn's hand now rested on the syringe that held the botched vaccine; now it was 'freedom.'

…Wait?! … 'Freedom,' was this the word imposed by Amber's will, or did Evelyn really, truly believe that now? 'Health,' 'freedom,' …and you can leave your 'prison.' Words and phrases, began to line the cerebral part of her mind as it felt as if she had already picked up the syringe, but, in actuality, it was already being held by Amber and Evelyn's conjoined consciousness in unison.

…Their minds finally one…

…Then the lab door shot open as the parents finally, with concerned rage, rushed in with desperation. Tears filled their eyes, but the look on the father held more of a stern face of fear and concern than that of the mother that was more torn up by the erratic new behavior her daughter now coveted—being if it were of her own accord.

"Evelyn! Dear… Put down that syringe, honey. It's dangerous, and not meant for you," the father urged her with further desperation as he feared if he approached that his daughter would do something regrettable.

"Please, baby," said her mother, instinctively, and with a continuum of tears pouring down her cheeks.

"And why should I?" Unerringly, she questioned being a being of two— she was now whole…

"What do you mean, Evelyn, dear?" Her father became frantic as the mother held back her tears further, but to no avail. "That's a botched vaccine.

Put it down, now! Your body wouldn't be able to handle it. The reaction will be unfathomable, but we theorized your body would shut down... or worse."

His hands were extended out in desperation to calm his seemingly distraught daughter that now held the syringe right to her neck. His nerves ignited into a frenzy as he struggled to steady his breathing. His face tried to stay stern, but he neared shattering. His vision tainted with rims of black as he feared for his little girl's safety. He never foresaw such an outcome, yet his heart burst into a repetition that cascaded with all of his regrets.

...He had failed his daughters.

"I have been in a constant Hell, Father, as I longed for a life outside these walls—you've imprisoned me! And now seeing my sister, we were never free." Evelyn started tearing up, not sure if remorse for what she was about to do, or if she were just fed up with her life. She continued with an angerful look that collaborated with a sense of melancholy, "From the confines of this jar, I looked in—slowly—through the eyes of my sister as you brought me closer and closer to a realization that..." She trailed off a bit, but at this moment, it was clear that Evelyn wasn't the one in control anymore.

"Wait?!... A-Amber?" Her father barely muttered because this revelation broke him. He collapsed as he realized his daughter was gone. Now he had lost both. Experiencing the trauma like an ever-present reality like a life flashing before his eyes, but rather filled with recurring mistakes. He had grown silent as his wife was stricken with terror. This wasn't natural, but rather, was it paranormal, the puppeteering of Evelyn's soul?

"GIVE ME BACK MY DAUGHTER!!" her mother screamed.

"But Mommy, I am your daughter." Amber spoke so plainly but held a cocky smirk.

She wasn't wrong, and this broke the mother now because her desperation was futile. Then the father stood from his self-reflection, and spoke diplomatically, "Okay, so what now? What?... Are you going to claim the body of your sister now? You don't even know what that syringe will do to you. You may never be the same again, so please, Amb—sweetie, please put down that Godforsaken concoction, and we can be a family again… You, me, and your mom."

He was closing in for a hug to comfort his fractured daughter's persona, and hopefully gradually retrieve the mutagen she still held aggressively close to her jugular. But she had caught on, and that was the start of her retribution…

"Nice try, Father," she said as she swiftly thrusted the needle into her neck.

"NO!" Her father lunged toward her, but to no avail because it was impossible to close the space between them.

It was a tragic spectacle as a single tear fell from the daughter's cheek, symbolizing her fading psyche as she is devoured by the dominating mutation of her sister's mind melding into hers. She screeched violently for a second as she bursted into a festival of vegetation that claimed the basement lab in its entirety. Evelyn's remains scattered like a blast of crimson paint painting a mural of depravity as it trickles down the luscious vines that now stretched and impaled the now deceased parents.

The world filled with darkness that day, and what of Evelyn no longer remained. But the blood seeped into the vines like nourishment for life sprouted from death. As the vegetation spread like cancer through the household, an egg remained like a seed hidden among the brush. In the recesses of this tainted den, something manifested from the brash mind of a corrupted soul. A manmade terror now grew unnatural due to flawed experimentation, but what was once dead in body now was alive in mind as this malicious entity consumed her sister, and they melded into a vessel growing beneath a world unaware.

As the environment grew poisonous to breath due to the toxins of the vegetative black mold that corroded the walls like rust, the compilation of the spore inside pulsated revealing new life, and so it opened like a Venus Flytrap from four petals that intersected at the top of the incubator of this monstrosity. The mucilage was evident as the petals parted, and inside peered a black abyss, but also from that darkness peered back a pair of eyes born from rage.

…And these eyes laid within the cranium of the sisters' made whole, a hybrid of blood and bone, and foliage that bring terror on this blasphemous world…

…but for now, she must feast…

Acknowledgments

It's been a long road in the making of this compendium. Most of my stories came from the sleeplessness of the mind as my ideas surged at night—mostly along the hour of midnight. I'd picture the horrors that lurked in the shadows, faces peering through my fascination. I also was inspired by the fears of others like my ex's fears of losing her sister in Kanji.

But I believe my greatest aspiration came from my family and friends that encouraged me by wanting to read my works. If I weren't inspired at the age of five, I don't know where I'd be, or if I would have ever written to begin with. I began drawing comics, which leapt a great deal after I was tortured at a young age. The adults around me saw a great deal of joy out of my pain as they sat me in front of horror games and movies.

These forms of media entertainment ignited a passion of sick pleasure from the adrenaline one would feel towards getting frightened. I'd laugh—I'd feel pleased if I were terrorized properly from the visuals I endured because I loved it! Such behaviors ignited the intention to bring said joy to others, so I thought to expand into horror.

I began writing back when I was five, and I had kept practicing since then until the day I felt adequate enough. I may have won awards, or ended up in a newspaper, but I thrived on the ideal of being a published author. I felt limited as a fledgling, but I kept writing. And now in adulthood, I succeeded where others could only dream, but dreams are reality with a little hard work.

So after achieving my aspiration, there is only striving for a career in writing as it is my life goal. I would like to thank those by name, the ones who have helped since I was a young fledgling, or to those I promised. I'll begin with those long departed…

The Departed:

I'd like to thank members of my family, and those that still linger in the heart: my brother, Toby (who will never be forgotten), and my grandfather, Carl (he was a real family man, and veteran to our great nation). And finally, to the one I promised I'd dedicate my first book to (never forgetting because I cared for this woman when I was little), my middle-school English teacher, Ms. Brown (who was taken in her prime).

The Encouraging:

Now to thank those still with me. I would begin with the obvious—family. If it weren't for my family fostering my talent and encouraging me, I couldn't imagine what I would be doing with myself today: my mother, Carol (which I stood by her side as well through tough times), my siblings (Sammy, Jade, Lilly, Zack, and Lexi—as not to exclude any of them), my grandmother, Joan (she was also very encouraging, even though she didn't always agree with my style).

• • •

And now, a special thanks to all my lovely Psychotics. If it weren't for the fans, I would have thought this not. I love writing, but the thought of my fellow horror lovers not receiving their prize after encouraging me this whole time would be cruel—so, this book is also dedicated to you. And I hope this book was to your liking, and I plan to bring more as soon as more become available…

. . .

And thank you all once again...
Until next time, my lovely Psychotics.